W9-CDK-998

BELLE STARR AND AN IMPOSTOR NAMED STARBUCK . . .

"Miz Belle, I do admire a modest lady. You make me proud to say I'm an ole Missouri boy. Yessir, you shorely do!"

"Have a seat." She waved him to a crude dining table. "I'll be with you in a minute."

Belle merely nodded and walked swiftly from the room. Outside, she wheeled right and strode to the end of the porch. Her husband, Sam, was stationed where he could watch the door, the shotgun cradled in one arm. His view through the window was partially obstructed by the angle, but he could see the edge of the dining table and Starbuck's hat. Belle stopped, fixing him with an annoyed squint. Her voice was harsh, cutting.

"What's your problem?"

"Not me," Sam grunted coarsely. "That feller in there's the problem."

"If you've got something to say, why don't you just spit it out?"

"You ain't gonna like it."

"Try me and see."

"We got to kill him, Belle. Kill him now!"

Books by Matt Braun

Black Fox
Bloody Hand
Buck Colter
Cimarron Jordan
Hangman's Creek
Jury of Six
Noble Outlaw
The Manhunter
Mattie Silks
The Savage Land
The Spoilers
Tombstone

Published by POCKET BOOKS

#5 MATT
BRAUN

THE
MANHUNTER

PUBLISHED BY POCKET BOOKS NEW YORK

Another *Original* publication of POCKET BOOKS

**POCKET BOOKS, a Simon & Schuster division of
GULF & WESTERN CORPORATION
1230 Avenue of the Americas, New York, N.Y. 10020**

Copyright © 1981 by Matthew Braun

ISBN: 0-671-41992-7

First Pocket Books printing September, 1981

10 9 8 7 6 5 4 3 2 1

POCKET and colophon are trademarks of Simon & Schuster.

Printed in the U.S.A.

To
BESS AND PAUL
WHOSE BELIEF AND SUPPORT
ARE BEYOND MEASURE

AUTHOR'S NOTE

The Old West produced a unique collection of rogues and rascals.

Outlaws and grifters, gunfighters and gamblers, they formed a roll call unsurpassed for shady exploits. Certain of these men were supreme egotists, actively courting fame and glory. They manipulated the media of the day, and the media, with a public clamoring for larger-than-life heroes, was delighted to oblige. Dime novelists, abetted by newspapers and periodicals, transformed these rogues and rascals into the stuff of legend. Later, with a remarkable disdain for the facts, movies and television added their own brand of hype to an already false mythology. The end result was a pantheon of stalwart gunmen and chivalrous desperadoes.

For the most part, it was folklore founded on invention and lies. And it was sold to America by hucksters with an uncanny knack for distorting the truth.

Jesse James was one of the myths fobbed off on a gullible public. Far from the Robin Hood of legend, he was a paranoid outcast who robbed banks and trains rather than work for a living. He was also a master of propaganda. Throughout his career as an outlaw, he wrote articulate and persuasive letters to the editors of several midwestern newspapers. The letters were duly reprinted, and accounted, in large measure, for the belief that he "robbed the rich and gave to the poor." In reality, he was something less than charitable; there is no documented instance of his assisting the needy or championing the cause of oppressed people. He was, moreover, a sadistic killer without mercy or remorse.

Still, Jesse James captured the public's imagination, and he did it with a certain flair. He was his own best press agent.

Yet every myth has some foundation in fact. The Old West produced many mankillers who were both honorable and courageous. For the most part, however, they shunned the limelight. Because they weren't seeking fame or immortality, they made poor source material for dime novelists and hack journalists. The upshot was that their attributes were grafted onto the rogues and rascals. America, as a result, ended up revering men who deserved no place in our folklore. The truly legendary characters of the era became little more than footnotes in the pages of history.

Luke Starbuck was one such man. His character is a composite of several Old West detectives, who were the most feared mankillers of the day. They worked undercover—generally in disguise—and thus their exploits are not widely known. In *The Manhunter* Starbuck accepts an assignment that pits him against Jesse James. Though the events depicted are historically accurate, certain liberties have been taken regarding time and place. Yet the characters are real, and the revelations unearthed by Starbuck are fact, not fiction. His investigation at last brings to light the truth about Jesse James. A hundred years overdue, it is nonetheless a story that needs telling.

The Manhunter also reveals Starbuck's role in the death of Jesse James. A compelling tale, it was until now shrouded in mystery. Luke Starbuck told no one of the part he played. For he was a man of many parts and many faces. None of them his own.

Chapter One

The men rode into town from the north. Their horses were held to a walk and they kept to the middle of the street. Unhurried, with three riders out front and two more trailing behind, they proceeded toward the center of town. No one spoke.

The community, like many midwestern farm towns, was bisected by a main thoroughfare. The business district, small but prosperous, consisted of four stores, a saloon and a blacksmith shop, and one bank. There were few people about and little activity in the downtown area. A typical Monday morning, it was the slowest time of the week. Which, in part, accounted for the five riders. Their business was better conducted in confidence and without crowds.

The men were unremarkable in appearance. Neatly dressed, they wore drab woolen suits and slouch hats. Three were clean-shaven and the other two sported well-trimmed beards. All of them were above average height, but only one, somewhat large and burly, was noticeable for his size. Their mounts were an altogether different matter. At first glance, the animals appeared to be common saddle stock. On closer examination, however, a uniform sleekness and conformation became apparent. The horses were built for endurance and stamina, staying power over long distances.

In the center of town, the riders wheeled to the left and halted before the bank. There was a military precision to their movements, smooth and coordinated, somehow practiced. The two bearded men stepped down and handed their reins to the third man in the front rank. Without hesitation, the two riders in the rear positioned their mounts to cover the street in both directions. A moment passed while one of the bearded men took a long look around. His bearing was that of a field commander and he subjected the whole of the business district to a slow, careful scrutiny. Then, followed by his companion, he turned and entered the bank.

Inside the door, he stopped and quickly scanned the room. The cashier's window and the vault were to the rear. He noted that the vault door was closed and, to all appearances, locked. To his immediate left, seated behind a desk, the bank president was engaged in conversation with three middle-aged men. By their dress and manner of speech, they were gentlemen landowners and therefore no threat. He pulled a .45 Smith & Wesson revolver from a shoulder holster inside his suit jacket.

"Get your hands up! Keep 'em up and you won't get hurt!"

There was an instant of leaden silence. The cashier froze, watching him intently. At the desk, the president stared at him with disbelief, and the three customers swiveled around in unison. Suddenly, eyes wide with terror, one of them panicked and bolted from his chair.

"Robbers! The bank's being robbed!"

A gun exploded and the man staggered, clutching

at his arm. His face went ashen, then he passed out, collapsing at the kness, and dropped to the floor. One eye on the cashier, the gang leader glanced over his shoulder. His companion, standing just inside the doorway, held a pistol trained on the men at the desk. A wisp of smoke curled upward from the barrel.

"Goddamnit!" he said gruffly. "Did you have to shoot him?"

"Seemed like the thing to do. Leastways it made him close his trap."

"Maybe so," the gang leader snapped. "But that gunshot will draw a crowd just sure as hell."

"I don't recollect that ever stopped you before."

"All right, forget it! Keep them birds covered while I tend to business."

With that, he walked to the rear of the bank and stopped before the cashier's window. He casually rested the butt of the Smith & Wesson on the counter, and nodded to the cashier.

"What's your name?"

"Martin," the cashier muttered. "Robert Martin."

"Well, Mr. Martin, how would you like to make it home to supper tonight?"

"I'd like that."

"Then get busy and open that vault. No fool tricks or I'll blow your head off. Hop to it!"

Martin eyed him steadily a moment, then turned toward the vault. A roar of gunfire, several shots in rapid succession, suddenly sounded from outside. The gang leader looked around and saw his companion peering out the door.

"What's all that about?"

"Nothin' serious. Some of the locals got nosy and the boys warned them to stay off the street."

"Keep a sharp lookout."

Turning back, he started and let loose a harsh grunt. Robert Martin had the cash drawer open and was clawing frantically at a revolver hidden beneath a stack of bills. The gang leader pulled the trigger and his Smith & Wesson spat a sheet of flame. The slug punched through Martin's forehead and tore out the back of his skull. A halo of bone and brain matter misted the air around his head, and he stood there a moment, dead on his feet. Then he folded at the waist and slumped to the floor.

"Dumb bastard!" the gang leader cursed savagely. "Told you I'd blow your head off!"

Leaning across the counter, he began scooping bills out of the cash drawer and stuffing them into his pockets. Once the drawer was empty, he wheeled about and marched toward the front of the bank. He signaled the bearded man at the door.

"Let's go! We're all done here."

"What about the vault?"

"No time! Another couple of minutes and the whole town'll be up in arms."

"The boys won't like it. They rode a long ways for a payday."

"Tough titty!" he barked. "You should've thought of that before you got an itchy trigger finger. C'mon, let's clear out!"

The din of gunfire swelled as they moved through the door. Still mounted, the gang members outside were winging random shots through store windows along the street. The merchants and townspeople had taken cover, and as yet there was no return fire. Crossing the broadwalk, the bearded men hastily swung into their saddles. Then, with everyone mounted, the robbers reined about and rode north out of town.

A short distance upstreet the gang leader abruptly brought his horse to a halt. Where the business district ended, the residential area began, and both sides of the street were lined with modest homes. Outside one house, a teenage boy stood at the edge of the yard. His eyes were filled with a mix of fear and youthful curiosity. He watched with wonder as the rest of the robbers skidded to a stop and turned their mounts. The gang leader calmly drew his pistol and extended it to arm's length. He stared down the sights at the boy.

"Come out to get an eyeful, did you?"

The youngster swallowed, licked his lips. "I didn't mean no harm, mister."

"Your mama should've taught you better manners."

Thumbing the hammer on his pistol, the gang leader sighted quickly and fired. A brilliant red splotch appeared on the pocket of the boy's shirt. He reeled backward, then suddenly went limp and fell spread-eagled in the yard. As he hit the ground, the other bearded robber kneed his horse forward, blocking the gang leader.

"Why'd you do that? Why'd you kill him?"

"I felt like it."

"For God's sake, he's just a kid!"

"So what."

"So what! You took your spite out on a kid. That's what!"

"Watch your mouth."

"The hell I will!"

The burly rider reined his horse closer. "What's the matter, Frank?"

"Ask Jesse."

"I'm askin' you."

"We didn't finish the job! Jesse said there wasn't time to clean out the vault, and now he's mad at himself."

"Wasn't time?" The large man scowled, turned his gaze on the gang leader. "Then how come you had time to stop and kill that kid?"

"Don't push me, Cole."

"And don't you try throwin' your weight around! We didn't ride to hell and gone just to come away with chicken feed."

"I told you to lay off! I won't tell you again."

"Well, I'll damn sure tell you something! Me and the boys are gonna go back and empty that vault. You can come or stay as you please."

"I'm warning you—!"

"Jesse, one of these days you're gonna warn me oncet too often."

A shot cracked and they instinctively ducked as a slug whizzed past their heads. Looking around, they saw a man standing in the middle of the street downtown. He had a rifle thrown to his shoulder, and as he fired the second time other men rushed to join him. The gang leader booted his horse and rapped out a sharp command.

"Too late now! Let's ride!"

A barrage from downtown settled the matter. With lead whistling around their ears, the robbers bent low and kicked their mounts into a headlong gallop. Moments later they cleared the edge of town and thundered north along a rutted wagon road.

Their leader, well out in front, never once looked back.

Chapter Two

Starbuck wiped his razor dry and walked from the bathroom. He selected a fresh linen shirt from the bureau, then took a conservative brown suit from the wardrobe. After knotting his tie, he slipped into a suit jacket and checked himself in the mirror. No dandy, he was nonetheless particular about his appearance.

Turning from the mirror, he moved to the bed and took a .45 Colt from beneath the pillow. He shoved the gun into a crossdraw holster worn on his left side, positioned directly above the pants pocket. The holster was hand-sewn and wet-molded to the Colt, crafted in such a manner that his belt snugged it flat against his body. The natural drape of his jacket concealed the entire rig and eliminated any telltale bulge. Only those who knew him well were aware that he went armed at all times.

Fully dressed, he walked toward the door leading to the sitting room. His suite in the Brown Palace Hotel was comfortable, though modest in size, and handsomely appointed. Off and on, after establishing headquarters in Denver, he had debated buying a house. His detective business kept him on the move—often for months at a stretch—and the cost of maintaining a suite on a permanent basis sometimes seemed exorbitant. Yet a house would have tied him down, and he wasn't a man who formed attachments easily. Besides, the hotel provided room service and laundry, not to mention a certain freedom of movement. All things considered, he was satisfied with the arrangement. It somehow suited his style.

Entering the sitting room, he nodded to the girl and took a seat beside her on the sofa. A singer, her stage name was Lola Montana, and she was the star attraction at the Alcazar Variety Theater. She was also his current bed partner, and for the past few weeks she had slept over almost every night. Still, in his view, she was a pleasant arrangement, with no strings attached.

A room-service cart was positioned beside the sofa. Earlier, they had shared a breakfast of ham and eggs, topped off with sourdough biscuits and wild honey. Now, luxuriating over a cup of coffee, Lola sat with her legs tucked under the folds of a filmy peignoir. The swell of her breasts was visible through the sheer fabric and she noted his appreciative glance. She vamped him with an engaging smile.

"You look real spiffy this morning, lover."

"I sort of like your getup, too. Hides just enough to give a fellow ideas."

"Ooo?" She slowly batted her eyelashes. "I thought by now you knew all my secrets."

"Let's just say you showed me a few surprises last night."

She laughed a low, throaty laugh. "The way I remember it, you rang the bell a couple of times yourself."

"Worked out even, then, didn't it?"

"How so?"

" 'Cause you rung the ding-dong clean out of mine."

His bantering tone delighted her. Normally reserved, he was a man of caustic wit but little natural humor. Like everyone else in Denver, she knew he was a manhunter—by some accounts, a mankiller—and a detective of formidable reputation. Danger intrigued her, and from the outset she'd been captivated by the fact that he looked the part as well. Corded and lean, with wide shoulders and a muscular build, he stood six feet tall. His eyes were pale blue, framed by a square jaw and light chestnut hair, and he gave the uncanny impression of seeing straight through another person. She thought his look not so much cold as simply devoid of emotion. The quiet, impersonal look of a man who would kill quickly, and without regret.

Today, however, his manner seemed light, almost chipper. She took that as a good sign, and wondered if he'd decided to unbend a little, let her have a glimpse of the man beneath the hard exterior. She felt no real conviction that it was true, and yet . . . a girl could always wish.

"Why not take the day off?" She stretched like a cat, and gave him a beguiling grin. "We could just loaf around, and who knows—maybe I'd show you some more surprises."

"Don't tempt me," Starbuck said genially. "The day's already half gone, and I've got some errands that won't wait."

"You know what they say, all work and no play."

"That's a laugh! You've kept me so busy, I haven't hardly had time to tend to business."

"Detective business?" she inquired innocently. "Or monkey business?"

Starbuck cocked one ribald eye at her. "I'll give you three guesses, and the first two don't count."

"Mr. Mysterious himself!" She mocked him with a minxlike look. "Got a hot case cooking, honeybun? C'mon, you can tell Lola."

"Strictly back-burner," Starbuck said vaguely. "Nothing worth the telling."

She laughed spontaneously, in sheer delight. "You're one of a kind, Luke! I've just been told to butt out and damned if you didn't make me like it. That's real talent!"

"Ask me no questions and I'll tell you no lies."

Starbuck understood it was a game, lighthearted and meant in jest. Unlike many women he'd known, she wanted nothing of him. A good time and a few laughs —along with their romps in bed—were all she sought from the liaison. She possessed a kind of bursting vitality, and she seemed to have discovered the instant recipe for fun. Then, too, there were her physical attributes, which amounted to an altogether stunning package. She was smallish and compact, with coltish grace and a dazzling figure. Her features were mobile and animated, with a wide, sensual mouth, and her hair hung long and golden. She was impudent and puckish, with a sort of mischievous verve, and the tricks she brought to his bed never failed to amaze him. All in all, she was his kind of woman, sportive and undemanding, with no claims on tomorrow or the future. He thought it might last awhile.

"All right, lover," she said cheerfully. "Off to the races! Get your business done and we'll save our playtime for tonight."

"That sounds like a proposition."

"There's one way to find out."

"Then I reckon I'd better drop around to the theater tonight."

"You miss my show and you'll never find out! How's that for a proposition?"

"Best offer I've had today."

She leaned forward and brushed his lips with a kiss. "See you there?"

"Count on it."

Starbuck rose and walked to the foyer. He took a wide-brimmed Stetson from the closet, jammed it on his head, and then shrugged into his overcoat. When he stepped into the hall, Lola poured herself another cup of coffee and lounged back on the sofa. A slow kittenish smile touched the corners of her mouth.

Outside the hotel Starbuck turned onto Larimer Street. It was a bitter cold day, with savage winds howling down from the northwest. A metallic sky rolled overhead and snow flurries peppered his face. As he passed the police station, he pulled up the collar of his coat and stuck his hands in his pockets. With the wind pushing him along, he rounded the corner and headed directly across town.

Several minutes later he crossed Blake Street. His destination was a small shop wedged between a pool hall and a hardware store. On the window was a neatly lettered sign, chipped and fading with age.

DANIEL CAMERON
GUNSMITH
PISTOLS—RIFLES—SHOTGUNS

An overhead bell jing-a-linged as Starbuck hurried through the door. The walls along both sides of the shop were lined with racks of long guns, and toward the rear a glass showcase was filled with pistols. Beyond the showcase, a gray-haired man turned from a workbench at the sound of the bell. Starbuck brushed snow off his coat and moved down the aisle.

"Afternoon, Daniel."

"Well, Luke!" Cameron warmly shook his hand. "I was beginning to think you'd forgotten our project."

"No," Starbuck said equably. "Too many irons in the fire, that's all."

"So I've heard." Cameron let a sly smile cross his face. "Apparently Lola Montana is a full-time . . . avocation."

Starbuck grinned. "If that means she keeps me busy, you're right. Course, I wouldn't exactly call it a chore."

"No need to explain." Cameron lifted his hands in an

exaggerated gesture. "A man needs diversion! Enjoy it while you're young."

"I'm doing my damndest," Starbuck said with heavy good humor. "How're things with you? Any luck?"

"Luke, I think I'm onto something. Not precisely what we're after, but close. Very close."

"Tell me about it."

"I'll do better than that. Come along and judge for yourself."

A master gunsmith, Cameron possessed an innovative mind and an unquenchable thirst to explore. Always receptive to a challenge, he had agreed to tackle a problem posed by Starbuck. The bullets commonly available were efficient killers but poor manstoppers. An outlaw, though mortally wounded in a gunfight, would often live long enough to empty his pistol. What Starbuck wanted was a bullet that would stop the other man instantly, neutralize him on the spot and take him out of the fight. For the past several weeks, engrossed in the project, Cameron had experimented with radical new bullet designs. Today, he proudly demonstrated the end result.

In the back room of the shop, Cameron lined up three Colt .45 shells on a table. The first was a factory loading, with the standard round pug-nosed bullet. The next shell, loaded with Cameron's new design, had a slug with shoulders which gradually tapered to a flat nose. The last shell was unlike anything Starbuck had ever seen. In effect, Cameron had turned his new slug upside down and loaded it backward. The nose of the slug was now inside the casing, and the base, which was blunt and truncated, was now seated in the forward position. After a brief explanation, Cameron loaded the shells into a Colt sixgun.

Along the rear wall were arranged three bales of wet newspaper that had been tightly bound with rope. The distance was less than five yards, and each of the bales was marked with a bold X in the center. Cameron aimed and fired, shifting from one bale to another, splitting the X with each shot. Then he walked forward, followed by Starbuck, and cut the bales open with a jackknife. The experiment spoke for itself.

The standard pug-nosed bullet had penetrated three-quarters of the way through the first bale. The bullet was virtually unmarred and still retained its original shape. The flat-nose slug, which was slightly deformed, had penetrated more than halfway through the second bale. Within the third bale, the reverse-loaded slug had penetrated scarcely one-third of the way through the wet newspaper. Yet the truncated base, upon impact with the bale, had been deformed beyond recognition. The entire slug had expanded, squashed front to rear, and emerged a mushroom-shaped hunk of lead.

"Quite an improvement," Cameron said, holding the slug between his fingertips. "The factory load expended all its energy drilling through the bale. Even my new design did much the same thing. But the reverse load! As you can see, the mushroom effect caused the bullet to impart its energy quickly and with massive shock."

Starbuck was impressed. "Would it work the same way on a man?"

"Much better," Cameron assured him. "The shock effect on human tissue would be far greater than it is on wet newsprint."

"Would it stop him cold?" Starbuck persisted. "Dead in his tracks?"

"Good question." Cameron's expression was abstracted. "I suppose we won't know that until you shoot someone, will we?"

"What about accuracy?"

"Now there we have a slight hitch. At long range, it's not as accurate as the factory load. On the other hand, most of your work is fairly close up. What would you estimate . . . five yards, ten at the outside?"

"I reckon it'd average that or less."

"Then you have no problem." Cameron tossed him

the slug. "Go try it on someone, Luke! I'm willing to bet it's a manstopper."

Starbuck left the shop with a box of the new shells in his overcoat pocket. His faith in Daniel Cameron, however, rode in the crossdraw holster on his belt. The Colt was now loaded with blunt-nosed slugs.

Starbuck's next stop was his office. Located around the corner from the Windsor Hotel, the office was a second-floor cubbyhole, with no sign on the door and spartan as a monk's cell. Essentially it was a clearinghouse, with a secretary to handle correspondence and light bookkeeping chores. All else, especially matters of a confidential nature, Starbuck committed to memory.

His secretary, Verna Phelps, greeted him with prune-faced civility. Her desk and chair, along with a battered file cabinet, were the only furnishings in the room. Her cool manner stemmed from the fact that she hadn't seen Starbuck in almost two weeks. Though Denver was a cosmopolitan city—with a population approaching 100,000—one of the holdovers from its frontier days was an active and highly efficient gossip mill. Almost from the start, she had known the unsavory details of Starbuck's latest dalliance. And in her most charitable moments she considered Lola Montana nothing short of a wanton hussy.

With no great urgency, Starbuck sifted through a stack of mail now several days old. One by one he dropped letters from various railroads, stagecoach lines, and mining companies on the desk. A man of means—with investments in commercial real estate and a portfolio of major stocks—he had no compelling financial need to work. Then, too, his reputation allowed him to accept only those assignments that piqued his interest.

Several of his previous cases were celebrated for the notoriety of the outlaws involved. He had been instrumental in ridding New Mexico of Billy the Kid, and largely through his efforts Wyatt Earp had been run out of Arizona. Apart from his eminence as a detective, he was also noted as a mankiller. By rough calculation—since he never discussed the topic—journalists estimated he had killed at least eighteen men. As a result, his fame had spread across the West, and he could now pick and choose from among the jobs offered. Yet fame, with the attendant publicity and newspaper photos, had destroyed the anonymity he'd once enjoyed. These days, he operated undercover, and always in disguise.

One letter caught his interest. Postmarked St. Louis, it was signed by the president of the International Bankers Association. Short and somewhat cryptic in tone, it requested his presence in St. Louis at the earliest possible date. He studied the letter a moment, then stuck it into his pocket. Looking up, he indicated the stack of mail he'd dropped on the desk.

"Write those outfits and tell them I'm unavailable till further notice."

A spinster, Verna Phelps had plain dumpling features and her hair was pulled severely away from her face into a tight chignon. She heartily applauded Starbuck's work as a detective, and took a certain grim satisfaction in the number of outlaws he'd killed. Yet she disapproved of his personal life, and viewed his conduct with women as reprehensible. Now, with a dour nod, she shuffled the letters into a neat pile.

"Are you accepting the St. Louis offer?"

"Maybe," Starbuck said noncommittally. "All depends on what they've got in mind."

"How long will you be gone?"

Starbuck shrugged. "Look for me when you see me."

"Very well." Her voice was tinged with reproach. "And the hotel suite? Shall I look after it as usual, or will your lady friend be staying on while you're gone?"

"Never give up, do you, Verna?" Starbuck smiled, and shook his head. "Follow the usual routine. Have the suite spruced up and tell the desk to send any messages over to you."

"Just as you wish, Mr. Starbuck."

"Hold down the fort." Starbuck waved, turning toward the door. "I'll be in touch."

Verna Phelps gave a rabbity sniff and watched him out the door. She marveled at his devilish ways and his taste for cheap, tawdry women. Then, blushing beet red, she was jolted by a sudden thought.

She wondered how it might have been . . . if she were younger.

Starbuck arrived at the Alcazar Variety Theater late that evening. The owner greeted him warmly, and escorted him to his usual table down front. A complimentary bottle of champagne materialized, and he settled back to enjoy the show.

Several men, seated at nearby tables, exchanged friendly nods. But no one attempted to approach Starbuck, or engage him in coversation. A private man, he tolerated few questions. Nor would he indulge drunks or the idly curious. He was known on sight, and what he did for a living was no secret. Still, though he was widely admired, he never spoke of his business to anyone. That too was known, and while some people considered it eccentric, his wishes were respected. The sporting crowd of Denver had long ago learned to take him on his own terns. Or not at all. Which suited him all the way around. He was alone even in the largest crowd.

Tonight, a solitary figure lost in his own thoughts, his mind centered wholly on the moment. Tomorrow he would entrain for St. Louis, and whatever happened would happen, all in good time. Before tomorrow, there was one last night with Lola, and not an hour to be wasted. His anticipation was heightened all the more as the curtain rose and the orchestra struck up a catchy tune. Lola went prancing across the stage, her legs flashing and her breasts jiggling over the top of a peekaboo gown. The audience roared and she gave them a dazzling smile. Then her husky alto voice belted out across the hall.

"Oh, don't you remember sweet Betsy from Pike,
Crossed the great mountains with her lover Ike,
With two yoke of oxen, a large yellow dog,
A tall shanghai rooster and one spotted hog!"

Chapter Three

St. Louis itself was worth the trip.

Starbuck arrived on a blustery January evening. From Union Station, he took a hansom cab to one of the fashionable hotels on Olive Street. There he registered under an assumed name and gave San Antonio as his hometown. To all appearances, he was a well-to-do Texan visiting the big city on business.

A precautionary measure, the deception had by now become second nature. Only a couple of months past, the *Police Gazette* had done an article that labeled Starbuck the foremost mankiller of the day. He had no idea whether his notoriety extended as far eastward as Missouri. Yet he was a man who played the odds, and assumed nothing. Outside Denver, he always traveled under an alias.

After supper in the hotel dining room, he went for a stroll. St. Louis, with a population exceeding the half-million mark, was the largest city he'd ever visited. The downtown district was a hub of culture and commerce. Theaters and swank hotels, office buildings and banks and business establishments occupied several square blocks between Market Street and Delmar Boulevard. A sprawling industrial section, which had gravitated early to the river front, lay stretched along the levee. Steamboats were rapidly losing ground to railroads, and the city had developed into a manufacturing center for clothing, shoes, and various kinds of machinery. Still, for all its advancement, St. Louis remained a major market for hides and wool, horses and mules, and a wide assortment of farm produce. However cosmopolitan, it had not yet fully made the transition from its frontier origins.

On the waterfront, Starbuck stood for a long while staring out across the Mississippi. The Eads Bridge, completed only eight years before, spanned the great river like a steel monolith. Far in the distance, he saw the lights of towns ranged along the Illinois shoreline. Not easily impressed, he was nonetheless taken with the sight. He had traveled the West from the Gulf of Mexico to the Pacific Coast, but he'd never had occasion to look upon the Mississippi. The breadth of the river, with girded steel linking one bank to the other, seemed to him a marvel almost beyond comprehension. He thought back to his days on the Rio Grande, and slowly shook his head. Age and experience, he told himself, altered a man's perception of things.

A nomadic westerner, Starbuck had grown to manhood in Texas. The Civil War, which had left him without family or roots, taught him that killing was a matter of expediency. Thereafter, he accepted abuse from no man, and quickly accommodated those who overstepped themselves. For a time he drifted from ranch to ranch, a saddletramp beckoned onward by wanderlust. Then, all within a period of a few years, he went from trailhand to ranch foreman to range detective. Quite by coincidence, one job leading to another, he discovered his niche in life.

Once his reputation as a manhunter spread, Starbuck branched out from chasing horse thieves and common rustlers. Offers from stagelines and railroads afforded greater challenge, and there he came into his own as a detective. Despite his renown, however, he was never really satisfied with yesterday's accomplishments. He enjoyed what he did for a livelihood, and he took pride in his work. Yet something of the old wanderlust still remained. He forever sought greater challenges, and he was cursed with an itch to move on to the next case. A blooded hunter, his quarry was man. And only when the chase was joined was he truly content.

Now, his gaze fixed on the Mississippi, he wondered what tomorrow would bring. His wire had confirmed the time and place for the meeting. Otis Tilford, president of the International Bankers Association, was expecting him first thing in the morning. An assessment would be made, and assuming he passed muster, an assignment would be offered. The only imponderable was whether or not he would accept. He was looking for tomorrows, not yesterdays, and nothing else would turn the trick. Nothing and no-damn-body.

He turned from the wharves and walked toward his hotel.

The Merchants & Farmers Bank Building stood on the corner of Fourth and Delmar. Starbuck entered the lobby shortly before nine o'clock and took an elevator to the third floor. At the end of the hall, he spotted a door with frosted glass and gilt lettering. He moved directly along the corridor, observant and suddenly alert. The lettering on the door was sparkling fresh.

Inside the waiting room he closed the door and doffed his hat. A mousy-looking woman, with gray hair and granny glasses, sat behind a reception desk. She looked him over, stern as a drill sergeant, and nodded.

"May I help you?"

"I'm Luke Starbuck. I have an appointment with Mr. Tilford."

"Yes, of course." She rose, bustling around the desk. "Please have a seat, Mr. Starbuck. I'll inform Mr. Tilford you're here."

Starbuck watched as she hurried down a hallway. Then, still standing, he slowly inspected the waiting room. All the furniture, including the receptionist's desk and a couple of wingbacked chairs, looked as though it had been delivered only that morning. A door on the opposite side of the room was open, and through it he saw several clerks in what appeared to be a general office. Their desks and a row of file cabinets along the far wall also looked fresh off a showroom floor. Whatever he'd expected, something about the layout put him on guard. He made mental note to do lots of listening, play it close to the vest. And volunteer nothing.

The receptionist reappeared, motioning him forward. "Will you come this way? Mr. Tilford can see you now."

"Much obliged," Starbuck said pleasantly. "I was just admiring your offices. Got a real handsome setup."

"Thank you."

"Been here long?"

"I beg your pardon?"

"Well, everything looks so new and all. I thought maybe you'd just opened for business?"

"No." She did not elaborate. "This way, Mr. Starbuck."

Starbuck followed her down the hall. She ushered him into a spacious office and stepped aside. The room was paneled in dark wood, with ornately carved furniture and a plush carpet underfoot. A coal-burning fireplace glowed cherry red, and directly opposite was an imposing walnut desk. Behind it, seated in a tall judge's chair, was a man who looked like a frog perched on a toadstool. He was completely bald, with a wattled neck and beady eyes, and his oval face was peppered with liver spots. When he rose, extending his hand, his posture was shrunken and stooped. Yet, oddly enough, his voice was firm and lordly.

"Welcome to St. Louis, Mr. Starbuck."

"Pleasure's all mine, Mr. Tilford."

"Please be seated." Tilford let go his hand, and dropped into the judge's chair. "I trust your trip was without incident."

"More or less." Starbuck took an armchair before the desk. "One train ride's pretty much like another."

"No doubt." Tilford appeared to lose interest in the subject. "I appreciate your quick response to our request."

"When a man says 'urgent,' I take him at his word."

"Commendable," Tilford said, no irony in his tone. "All the more so since your services are much in demand these days."

"Don't believe everything you read in the *Police Gazette*."

Tilford's laugh was as false as an old maid's giggle. "On the contrary, Mr. Starbuck! I found the article most informative. Few men have your zeal."

"Oh?" Starbuck asked casually. "How so?"

"Once you accept a case, you display a remarkable tendency to see it through to a conclusion. Would you consider that a fair statement?"

"I generally finish what I start."

"Precisely." Tilford gave him an evaluating glance. "And more often than not you finish it permanently. Correct?"

Starbuck regarded him thoughtfully. "Why do I get the feeling you know the answer before you ask the question?"

"I too am a man of zeal," Tilford replied loftily. "I had you checked out thoroughly before sending that wire."

"Sounds reasonable." Starbuck smiled humorlessly. "Hope you got your money's worth."

"The queries were of a personal nature. A man in

my position develops certain alliances, and we often exchange information. All on a confidential basis, of course."

"Anyone I know?"

"What's in a name?" Tilford spread his hands in a bland gesture. "Suffice it to say you come highly recommended by the Central Pacific and Wells, Fargo."

"I reckon they had no room for complaint."

"Indeed!" Tilford wagged his head. "You are too modest by far, Mr. Starbuck. I am reliably informed that you have no equal when it comes to meting out justice to outlaws."

"There's all kinds of justice."

"True." Tilford pursed his lips and nodded solemnly. "But only one kind of any lasting value. Wouldn't you agree, Mr. Starbuck?"

Starbuck took out the makings and rolled himself a smoke. He struck a match, all the while watching Tilford, and lit the cigarette. Then, inhaling deeply, he settled back in his chair.

"Suppose we get down to cases?"

"By all means." Tilford leaned forward, stared earnestly at him. "I presume you are familiar with the James-Younger gang?"

Starbuck looked at him without expression. "Jesse James?"

Tilford made a small nod of acknowledgment. "Over the last seventeen years James and his gang have robbed dozens of banks and trains—"

"So I've heard."

"—and killed at least a score of innocent people."

"I wouldn't argue the figure."

"And yet," Tilford said in an aggrieved tone, "they are free to come and go as they please throughout Missouri."

"I understood," Starbuck observed neutrally, "that the Pinkertons had been brought in on the case."

"Quite true." Tilford's eyelids drooped scornfully. "Some eight years ago the Pinkerton Agency was retained for the express purpose of putting a halt to these depredations."

"That long?" Starbuck blew a plume of smoke into the air. "Guess they've had a run of bad luck."

"You're too charitable," Tilford said, not without bitterness. "To put it bluntly, Allan Pinkerton has accomplished nothing—absolutely nothing!—and he has been paid very handsomely for doing it."

"Nobody's perfect," Starbuck commented dryly. "Maybe it's time for the worm to turn."

"I seriously doubt it." Tilford shook his head in exasperation. "A coalition of banks and railroads still has Pinkerton under retainer. In my view, however, it's a waste of money. Given another eight years, he would be no closer than he is today."

"Sounds like you hold the Pinkertons in pretty low opinion."

"Unless I'm mistaken"—Tilford watched him carefully—"that is an opinion we share, Mr. Starbuck."

Starbuck flipped a hand back and forth. "Let's just say I think they're a little bit overrated."

"How would you like an opportunity to prove your point?"

"Try me and see."

"Very well." Tilford's voice dropped. "We wish to retain your services, Mr. Starbuck. Within reasonable limits, you can name your own price."

"Exactly what services did you have in mind?"

Tilford's face took on a sudden hard cast. "We want Jesse James killed."

Starbuck's gaze was direct now, his ice-blue eyes alert. "Who is 'we'?"

"Why, the International Bankers Association. I thought you understood—"

"Try another tune." Starbuck fixed him with that same disquieting stare. "The lettering on your door looks like the paint's hardly had time to dry. Every stick of furniture in your office is brand new, and unless I miss my guess, so's your association." He paused, his eyes cold and questing. "I'll ask you again, and this time I want some straight talk. Who is 'we'?"

A shadow of irritation crossed Tilford's features. "You are a very discerning man, Mr. Starbuck. I commend you on your powers of observation. However, I am not in the habit of being interrogated. Nor do I appreciate your rather cavalier manner."

"That's your problem," Starbuck said woodenly. "Either I get an explanation or we don't do business. Take your pick."

Tilford reflected a moment. "Very well," he answered at length. "A number of bankers around the Midwest deplore Pinkerton's lack of results. We have severed our ties with the railroad and banking coalition, and formed our own organization. Our purpose is legitimate and quite straightforward. We intend to eradicate Jesse James and those of a similar persuasion."

"How do you fit into the picture?"

"I am president and chief stockholder of the Merchants and Farmers Bank. In short, I own the bank downstairs and the building in which we are seated."

Starbuck played a hunch. "From what I've heard, James normally concentrates on small-town banks. So that lets you out, unless you've got some personal score to settle. Suppose you tell me about it?"

"Are you a mind reader as well as a detective, Mr. Starbuck?"

"Tricks of the trade," Starbuck said flatly. "I'm waiting for an answer."

Tilford regarded him somberly. "Last July the evening train out of Kansas City was robbed. The conductor and a passenger by the name of McMillan were murdered in cold blood. Jesse James, and his brother Frank, were positively identified as the killers. Frank McMillan was my son-in-law."

"Tough break." Starbuck stubbed out his cigarette in an ashtray. "Any special reason you took it so personal?"

"I sent Frank to Kansas City on business. He was an officer of this bank, the husband of my only daughter, and the father of my grandchildren. As should be obvious, I feel responsible for his death."

"In other words," Starbuck ventured, "you want an eye for an eye. You formed the association—and gave it a high-sounding name—in order to put a legitimate front on personal vengeance."

"Not altogether," Tilford countered. "By ridding society of Jesse James, I am also performing a public service. I see those as compatible goals—a worthy endeavor!"

"Why kill him?" Starbuck inquired. "Why not bring him to trial and let him hang? That way the state executes him . . . instead of you."

"He must be killed!" Tilford's voice was heated and vindictive. "No jury in this state would convict Jesse James. Nor would any court dare impose the death penalty."

"What makes you so sure?"

Tilford rose and moved to the wall directly behind him. With some effort, he lifted a large leather satchel off the floor and dropped it on his desk. Then, his expression grim, he resumed his chair.

"Inside that satchel you will find the Pinkerton file—eight years of investigation and surveillance—on the James-Younger gang. I obtained a duplicate of the file in the hope it would speed your own investigation. Aside from that, it will also convince you that Jesse James can never be convicted in the state of Missouri."

"Out of curiosity"—Starbuck gave him a quizzical look—"how did you come by it?"

"A friend," Tilford explained. "One who owns a railroad and contributes large sums to the settlement of Allan Pinkerton's fee."

Starbuck studied the satchel, thoughtful. For most of his professional career he had lived in the shadow of the world's most famous detective agency. The idea of going head to head with the Pinkertons—and beating them—was a challenge he found too tempting to resist. At last, with an overdrawn gesture, he looked up at Tilford.

"I don't work cheap."

"Ten thousand now," Tilford said gravely, "and ten thousand more when the job is completed. With one added proviso."

"Which is?"

"You are to kill Frank James as well."

"Want your pound of flesh, don't you?"

"I want them dead, Mr. Starbuck! Dead and buried —and forgotten."

"Hell, why not?" Starbuck shrugged. "I reckon one deserves it as much as the other."

"Then we have an agreement?"

"You ante up and we're in business. Two for the price of one, delivery guaranteed."

"Where will you start?"

Starbuck smiled cryptically. "Where Pinkerton should have started."

"Oh?" Tilford appeared bemused. "Where might that be?"

"Let's just say it won't be out in the open."

Chapter Four

The Pinkerton file was compelling stuff. Starbuck found himself fascinated almost from the first field report, which was dated January 23, 1874. He also found confirmation of what he'd suspected all along.

Jesse James was no garden-variety outlaw.

For three days and nights, Starbuck holed up in his hotel room. The file, he determined early on, could not be let out of his sight. One look by a snooper would jeopardize the need for secrecy, and pose the even greater threat of a leak to the press. Accordingly, he refused to allow the maids inside, and he himself never set foot outside. All his meals were ordered from room service, and on the first night he sent a bellman to fetch a quart of whiskey. Like a monk sequestered in a cell, he was alone with himself. And the file.

His first chore was to devise some system of organization. The file was voluminous, and from the outset it was apparent that Allan Pinkerton had a fondness for long, rambling memos. The agency's founder exhorted everyone in his employ—from division chiefs to field operatives—with page after page of detailed instructions regarding the investigation. The flow of paperwork was compounded by the sheer number of personnel involved in the case. Apart from Pinkerton's two sons, who were responsible for field operations, there were a dozen or more investigators active at all times. The avalanche of reports and memos, generated from different parts of the country, was stupefying to contemplate. A method was needed to separate the chaff from the wheat.

Starbuck broke the material down into categories. Allan Pinkerton's directives, which contained little of value, were consigned to an ever-growing pile. Speculative reports were next in line, and armchair analyses by division chiefs formed still another stack. On-the-scene reports, written by field operatives, were divided into those dealing with conjecture and those that dealt in hard intelligence. The latter category, scarcely to Starbuck's surprise, made up the smallest pile. Nevertheless, taken as a whole, the file provided an absorbing overview. Chronicled there was the violent history of the James-Younger gang.

Like many men brutalized by the Civil War, Jesse and Frank James found it difficult to adjust to peacetime. During the hostilities they had ridden with Quantrill's guerrillas, and those savage years had instilled in them a taste for action. Bored and restless, they avoided the family farm and made no effort to earn an honest livelihood. Quickly enough, they developed a reputation as the chief troublemakers of Clay County.

To make matters worse, the Federal occupation forces sought retribution against their defeated enemies. Yet the James brothers were in no greater danger of reprisals than the balance of Quantrill's ex-guerrillas. The vast majority of former Confederates settled down and went to work, determined to put the war behind them. Other men, however, felt society had turned on them, and that a life of robbery and murder was justified. Such was the backdrop against which Jesse and Frank James took the outlaw trail.

At the time, Jesse James was eighteen years of age. Still, for all his youth, he was a blooded veteran and an experienced leader of men. Headstrong, with magnetic force of character, he dominated Frank, who was three years his senior. The Younger brothers, who were boyhood friends and former comrades under Quantrill, were recruited into the gang. Cole Younger, the eldest of the four brothers, was the same age as Frank James. Yet, like Frank, he submitted to the will of a fiery young hothead. By late winter of 1865, the gang was formed, all of them ex-guerrillas and stone-cold killers. Their leader was Jesse James.

Only ten months after the civil War ended, the long string of depredations committed by the James-Younger gang began. On the morning of February 3, 1866, they rode into Liberty, Missouri, and robbed the Clay County Savings Association of $70,000. It was the first daylight bank robbery in American history, and created a furor in the nation's press. It also served as the template by which the gang would operate over the years ahead. In the course of the holdup, the bank teller and an innocent bystander were callously murdered. The only shots fired were those fired by the gang, and they escaped unharmed. The scene would be repeated time and time again.

For the next eight years the gang roamed the Midwest, robbing trains and looting banks. Their raids were conducted with military precision, and ranged over an area encompassing Missouri, Kansas, Arkansas, Kentucky, and Iowa. The dead littering their backtrail grew in number with each holdup, yet pursuit was rare. Even though the law knew their names, no concerted effort was made to track them to their homeground in Missouri. Like will-o'-the-wisps they appeared from nowhere—hitting fast and hard—then vanished without a trace. And the bloodletting went on unabated.

Early in 1874 the Pinkerton agency entered the case. Their failure was monumental, and resulted in an immediate loss of prestige. One of their agents, operating undercover, was captured in Clay County. With his hands tied behind his back, he was executed personally by Jesse James. As an added humiliation—and a warning to all lawmen—his body was left to be savaged by wild hogs. The incident kindled in Allan Pinkerton an unyielding hatred for the outlaws. His memos thereafter took on the fevor and tone of a holy war.

A few months later Pinkteron suffered yet another loss of face. On a brisk March day, two operatives, accompanied by a deputy sheriff, were surprised by Jim and John Younger. The encounter occurred on a backcountry road, and in the ensuing shootout both Youngers were wounded. One of the detectives and the deputy sheriff were killed on the spot. The second Pinkerton escaped during the confusion, and thus lived to tell the tale. While John Younger ultimately died of his wounds, the message quickly made the rounds among peace officers. Any outsider who ventured into Clay County—whether Pinkerton or lawman—would be made to pay the price. And then left to the wild hogs.

In the end a combination of partisan politics and the terror inspired by the gang defeated the Pinkertons. If a group of former Quantrill raiders held up a bank or robbed a train, the common wisdom was that no great harm had been done. Bankers and railroad barons, who were considered thieves themselves, could easily afford the loss.

Friends and relatives, moreover, were always willing to hide the outlaws. Of no less significance, they also provided the gang with an efficient and highly reliable intelligence network. No stranger entered the backwoods of Clay County without arousing comment, and word swiftly found its way to those who supported the robbers. Those who were unsympathetic simply tended their own business and made every effort to remain neutral. Forced to choose, few would have taken sides with Yankee detectives in any event. A veil of silence hung like a wintry cloud over all of Clay County.

After losing two operatives, Allan Pinkerton waited almost a year before he again challenged the James boys on homeground. On the night of January 25, 1875, a squad of Pinkerton agents surrounded the home at the family farm. Jesse and Frank, with several members of the gang, had ridden away only hours before. Inside the house were Jesse's mother, his stepfather, Dr. Reuben Samuel, and his young half brother, Archie Samuel. A servant, awakened when the operatives pried open a window shutter, sounded the alarm.

The Pinkertons, determined to capture or kill the James boys, immediately tossed a large iron bomb through the window. While the family stumbled about in the dark, the bomb exploded. A piece of shrapnel struck Jesse's mother and tore off her right arm below the elbow. Across the room, young Archie was hit in the chest by another jagged shard and died instantly. Only the quick thinking of Dr. Samuel, who hastily applied a tourniquet to his wife's arm, saved her from bleeding to death.

With the house ablaze, and no sign of the James boys, the detectives panicked and fled. Later the Pinkerton agency denied that the object hurled through the window was a bomb. By then, however, the damage was done. Censure from the community and several prominent politicians forced Allan Pinkerton to withdraw his operatives from Clay County. Thereafter the Pinkertons were vilified as assassins and child killers. And the legend of Jesse James took on a whole new dimension.

Oddly enough, that aspect of the case stirred Starbuck's admiration. The Pinkerton file documented beyond question that Jesse James was a social misfit with a deep-rooted persecution complex. Nor was there any doubt that he was a mad-dog killer—lacking mercy or remorse—who dispatched his victims with cold ferocity. Yet he was also a master of propaganda. With cunning and calculation, he had captured the public's imagination and transformed himself into a heroic figure. In a very real sense, he was his own best press agent, and one with a certain flair for words. However grudgingly, Starbuck had to admit he'd done a slam-bang job of whitewashing himself and his murderous deeds.

Throughout the years, James had written articulate and persuasive letters to the editors of influential midwestern newspapers. The letters were duly reprinted, and accounted, in large measure, for the myth that "he robbed the rich and gave to the poor." Comparisons were drawn between Jesse James and Robin Hood, the legendary outlaw of Sherwood Forest. Not entirely in jest, newspaper editorials made reference to "Jesse and his merry band of robbers."

Apocryphal tales were widely circulated with regard to his charitable nature and his compassion for the poor. One story, typical of many, credited Jesse with donating a bag of gold to help establish a school for Negro children in Missouri. The gold, naturally, was reported to have been liberated from the coffers of a money-grabbing banker. In time, with such tales multiplying, Jesse became known as a champion of the oppressed and downtrodden. To backwoods Missourians and gullible Easterners alike he came to represent a larger-than-life figure. A Robin Hood reborn—who wore a sixgun and puckishly thumbed his nose at the law.

In Starbuck's view, the fault could be traced directly to the Pinkertons. Had they done their job, Jesse James would have been tried and hanged, and long forgotten, Instead they had botched the assignment from beginning to end. By hounding James for eight years they had turned themselves into the villains of the piece and transformed him into the underdog. Their abortive raid on the family farm had merely capped an already miserable performance. A child's death, and the horror of an innocent woman losing her arm, had been perceived by the public as unconscionable. That one act had stamped the Pinkertons as skulking cowards, somehow more outside the law than the man they hunted. And Jesse James, mindful of public reaction, had quickly seized on the opportunity. Without the Pinkertons, he would have been just another outlaw, foxier than most but nothing to rate front-page headlines. With the Pinkertons, he had become a mythical creature and a national sensation. A legend.

On the evening of the third day Starbuck finally put the file aside. His eyes were bloodshot from reading and his head felt like an oversoaked sponge. He poured himself a stiff shot of whiskey and slugged it back in a single motion. Then he stretched out on the bed, hands locked behind his head, and stared at the ceiling. Slowly, with infinite care, he examined what he'd gleaned from the file.

Several things were apparent now. Foremost among them was the fact that Otis Tilford had given him the straight goods. Nowhere in Missouri could Jesse James be tried in a court of law and found guilty. Even in the event he were captured, there was little likelihood of securing an indictment. The time for that was long past, and would never again return. Underdogs who became living legends were immune to the laws that governed lesser men. So the alternative was obvious, and precisely as Tilford had stated. Jesse James had to be killed.

Insofar as the job itself was concerned, Starbuck realized he faced a formidable task. All the obstacles that had defeated the Pinkertons would likewise hinder his own investigation. The people of Clay County were clannish, openly suspicious of any stranger, and would doubtless prove none too talkative. To compound the problem, they were rightfully fearful of the James-Younger gang, and aware of the consequences to anyone who spoke out of school. The reasonable conclusion, then, was that he would make little headway in Clay County itself. Without solid information—a lead of some sort—it would be a waste of time and effort. Not to mention the great probability he'd wind up bushwhacked on a back-country road some dark night.

Still, based on what he'd read in the file, there was a definite pattern to the gang's activities. After pulling a job every six months or so, they always vanished without a trace. Generally a month or longer would pass before they were again reported in Clay County. Which meant they went to ground and laid low following a holdup. The Pinkertons, even with their bureaucratic mentality, had tumbled to the pattern.

Yet, at the same time, the Pinkertons had overlooked what seemed a salient point. A passing comment in one of the reports noted that Cole Younger had sired a daughter by Belle Starr. Almost as an afterthought, the report indicated that Belle Starr was now living in Indian Territory. No other connection had been made regarding the gang, particularly with respect to Jesse James. Nor had it occurred to the Pinkertons to check it out further. Either Indian Territory wasn't their cup of tea, or else they considered the item a worthless bit of trivia. Whichever, it seemed to Starbuck an oversight.

There was a link, however tenuous, between Cole Younger and his former lady love. Coupled with the fact that the gang vanished after every job, it made for interesting speculation. Moreover, from the standpoint of a robber, it was a link that made eminent good sense. A hideout in Indian Territory would be damn hard to beat. Not only was it a sanctuary for outlaws, but the nearest law was the U.S. marshal's office at Fort Smith. No better place existed for a man to lose himself until the dust settled. And taken to its logical conclusion, the thought was equally true for an entire gang. Perhaps more so.

Starbuck had no idea whether Cole Younger and Belle Starr were still on speaking terms. That Jesse James and the gang used her place as a hideout was an even greater question mark. Yet the link existed, and thus far it was his only lead. A place to start.

Chapter Five

Starbuck stepped off the train at a whistle-stop in Indian Territory. A way station for travelers and freight, the depot was located on the west bank of the Arkansas River. On the opposite shore stood Fort Smith.

Hefting his warbag, Starbuck walked toward the ferry landing. No stranger to Indian Territory, he was reminded of an assignment that now seemed a lifetime ago. Some seven years past, on his first job as a range detective, he had trailed a band of horse thieves through the Nations. The homeland of the five Civilized Tribes—Cherokee, Chickasaw, Choctaw, Creek, and Seminole—it was so named because they had chosen to follow the white man's path. Bounded by Texas, Kansas and Arkansas, the Nations were still a long way from civilized.

No less ironic, in Starbuck's view, was the name of the railroad line. The Little Rock & Fort Smith Railroad extended to the depot on the western shoreline, and the river roughly paralleled the boundary separating Arkansas and Indian Territory. But there was no bridge spanning the river, and thus the railroad stopped short of its namesake. Ferryboats were the sole means of conveying freight and passengers from the depot to Fort Smith. As a practical matter, the railroad terminus was on Indian land, and separated from the white man's world by far more than a river. From the depot westward there was a sense of having taken a step backward in time.

Now, standing on the foredeck of the ferry, Starbuck stared across the river at Fort Smith. Originally an army post, the town was situated on a sandstone bluff overlooking the juncture of the Arkansas and Poteau rivers. With time, it had become a center of commerce and trade, serving much of western Arkansas and a good part of Indian Territory. Warehouses crowded the waterfront, and in the distance the town itself looked to be a prosperous frontier community. The largest settlement bordering the Nations, it boasted of four newspapers, one bank, and thirty saloons which enjoyed a captive trade from transients bound for the great Southwest. By federal law, the sale of firewater was banned throughout Indian Territory.

When the ferry docked, Starbuck inquired directions to the U.S. marshal's office. From the wharf, he followed Garrison Avenue, the main street that ran through the center of town. On the far side of the business district, he approached the garrison of the old army post. Abandoned some years before by the military, the compound was now headquarters for the Federal District Court of Western Arkansas. And the indisputable domain of Judge Isaac Charles Parker—the Hanging Judge.

Starbuck, like most Westerners, thought Judge Parker had been slandered by the Eastern press. His jurisdiction covered Western Arkansas and all of Indian Territory, a wilderness area which encompassed some 74,000 square miles. To enforce his orders, he was assigned two hundred U.S. deputy marshals, and the almost impossible task of policing a land virtually devoid of law. Four months after taking office, he had sentenced six convicted murders to be hanged simultaneously.

The thud of the gallows trap that day called the attention of all America to Judge Parker. Newspapermen poured into Fort Smith, and a crowd of more than 5,000 gathered to witness the executions. The press immediately tagged him the Hanging Judge, and decried the brutality of his methods. In the furor, the purpose of his object lesson was completely lost. Yet the reason he'd hung six men that day—and went on to hang eighteen more in the next six years—lay just across the river.

Gangs of white outlaws made forays into Kansas, Missouri, and Texas, and then retreated into Indian Territory. There they found perhaps the oddest sanctuary in the history of crime. Though each tribe had its own sovereign government, with courts and Light Horse Police, their authority extended only to Indian citizens. White men were untouchable, exempt from all prosecution except that of a federal court. Yet there were no extradition laws governing the Nations; federal marshals had to pursue and capture the wanted men; and in time the country became infested with hundreds of fugitives from justice. Curiously enough, the problem was compounded by the Indians themselves.

The red man had little use for the white man's laws, and the marshals were looked upon as intruders in the Nations. All too often the Indians connived with the outlaws, offering them asylum; and the chore of ferreting out entire gangs became a murderous task. It was no job for the faint of heart, as evidenced by the toll in lawmen. Over the past six years nearly thirty federal marshals had been gunned down in Indian Territory.

The old military garrison was a grim setting for the

grim work carried out by Judge Parker and his staff. A bleak two-story building housed the courtroom and offices for the federal prosecutors. As many as ten cases a day were tried, and few men were acquitted. The majority were given stiff sentences—all the law would allow—and quickly transported to federal prisons. Convicted murderers were allowed one last visit with immediate family. Then they were hung.

Another stone building, formerly the post commissary, was situated across the old parade ground. A low, one-story affair, it was headquarters for the U.S. marshal and his complement of deputies. In the center of the compound, within clear view of both buildings, stood the gallows. Constructed of heavy timbers, it had four trap doors, each three feet wide and twenty feet long. If occasion demanded, there was adequate space for twelve men to stand side by side and plunge to oblivion on the instant. The structure was roofed and walled, so that executions could be performed even in bad weather. Judge Parker, among other things, believed that justice should be swift—and timely.

Crossing the compound, Starbuck observed activity near the gallows. A crowd, growing larger by the minute, was gathering outside a roped-off area which formed a horseshoe around three sides of the structure. The onlookers were composed of townspeople and farmers, their wives and children, and a collection of travelers distinguishable by their dress. A holiday atmosphere seemed to prevail, and an excited murmur swept over them as a bearded man slowly mounted the stairs. Hushed, the spectators watched as he walked to the center trap and began testing the knotted hemp nooses. All business, he went about his work with an air of professional detachment.

Starbuck figured it was his lucky day. From the looks of things, he would get to see the Western District Court in action. With one last glance, he went up the steps to the old commissary building. Inside, directly off the hallway, he entered what appeared to be the main office. A man was seated at a battered roll-top desk, hunched forward over a litter of paperwork. He looked up without expression, and waited.

"Afternoon," Starbuck said amiably. "I'd like to see the U.S. marshal."

"You've found him," the man replied, rising from his chair. "I'm Jim Fagan."

Starbuck accepted his handshake. "Luke Starbuck."

Fagan was bearish in appearance, with square features and a shaggy mane of hair. Yet there was a rocklike simplicity in his manner, open and unassuming. He let go Starbuck's hand, cocked his head to one side.

"Starbuck," he repeated aloud. "Why, hell, yes! You're the detective fellow, aren't you? The one that got his picture in the *Police Gazette.*"

"Wish to Christ I hadn't," Starbuck admitted unhappily. "In my line of work, it don't pay to have your face plastered all over the country."

"Take a load off your feet." Fagan gestured to a chair beside the desk. "Not often we get a look at a real-live detective."

Starbuck seated himself. "Don't believe everything you read. Lots of that stuff was hogwash, pure and simple."

"Now you're gonna spoil my day! Near as I recollect, that article said you had a hand in puttin' the skids to Wyatt Earp and Billy the Kid. You mean to tell me it's not so?"

"No," Starbuck conceded. "I'm just saying reporters invent about half of what they write. Never known one yet that stuck to the straight facts."

"Guess you got a point." Fagan leaned back in his chair, suddenly earnest. "Well, now, what brings you to Fort Smith? Hot on a case, are you?"

"After a fashion," Starbuck commented. "Wondered what you could tell me about Belle Starr."

"What's to tell?" Fagan said with mild contempt.

"Her and Sam Starr—that's her husband—rustle livestock and pull penny-ante holdups. Strictly small-time."

"What kind of holdups?"

"Nuisance stuff," Fagan observed. "Trading posts, backwoods stores . . . every now and then they smuggle a load of whiskey into the Nations. Between them, they haven't got brains enough to take on a bank or train."

"Why haven't you arrested them?"

"We've got our hands full with the *real* hardcases. Course, that don't mean their number won't show. One of these days we'll get 'em for horse stealing or some such—only a matter of time."

"So there's nothing hanging over their heads right now?"

"Nothing particular." Fagan's gaze sharpened. "What's your interest in Miz Belle? She's a slut, common as dirt. Otherwise she wouldn't have married herself off to a reformed dog-eater."

"Her husband's an Indian?"

Fagan nodded. "Full-blooded Cherokee."

"I understand they've got a place over in the Nations."

"On the Canadian River," Fagan affirmed. "Way the hell back in the middle of nowhere. Not marked on any map, but it's called Younger's Bend."

Starbuck looked startled. "Younger's Bend?"

"Well, so the story goes, Belle had herself a kid by Cole Younger. That was some years ago, but apparently she's not one to forget an old sweetheart."

"You're saying she named her place after Cole Younger?"

Fagan slowly shook his head. "I can see how you made your mark as a detective. You've got a knack for askin' all the questions—without answering any yourself."

"No offense," Starbuck said, smiling faintly. "Old habits are hard to break."

"Suppose we try," Fagan said in a firm voice.

"You dodged it a minute ago, so I'll ask again. What's your interest in Belle Starr?"

Starbuck gave him a thoughful stare. "Anything I say would have to be off the record."

Fagan unpinned his badge and tossed it on the desk. "Shoot."

"I'm after Jesse and Frank James. I've got reason to believe they're using Belle Starr's place as a hideout."

"The hell you say!" Fagan looked at him with some surprise. "Where'd you get a notion like that?"

"A word here, a word there," Starbuck said evasively. "Nothing solid, but a man plays his best hunch."

"One way to find out," Fagan informed him. "I've got a chief deputy that sort of oversees the Cherokee Nation. Want me to call him in?"

"Will he keep his lip buttoned?"

"I'll guarantee it." Fagan threw back his head and roared. "Heck Thomas! Get your dusty butt in here —now!"

A moment passed, then the sound of footsteps drifted in from the hallway. The man who appeared through the door was tall and rangy, with close-cropped hair and a wide handlebar mustache. His eyes were gray and impersonal, and his features were set in the stern expression befitting a church deacon. Starbuck marked him as a mankiller, which immediately put them on common ground.

After a round of introductions, Fagan briefly explained the situation. Heck Thomas listened impassively, arms folded across his chest, saying nothing. At last, when his boss concluded, his gaze shifted to Starbuck.

"Belle and Sam aren't too high on our list, you understand?"

"So Marshal Fagan told me."

"Anything I pass along would be mostly hearsay and rumor."

"No harm in listening."

"Well—" Thomas paused, lifted his shoulders in a shrug. "Every now and then I get word that a bunch of strangers have been seen at Belle's place. Just that —a bunch of strangers—no names, no descriptions."

"You never had reason to check it out?"

"Nope," Thomas said simply. "Belle's probably screwed half the male population of Indian Territory. So it don't spark much curiosity when we hear there's strange men hangin' around her place."

"These strangers," Starbuck inquired, "were they white men?"

"I don't remember anybody sayin' one way or the other."

"How often have you heard they were there?"

"Oh, once or twice a year. Course, keep in mind, I never heard it was the same men every time. Like I said, no names, no descriptions . . . nothin'."

Starbuck thought it was far from nothing. The appearance of strangers at Belle Starr's place—once or twice a year—dovetailed very neatly with the disappearance of the James gang following their periodic holdups. The information was promising, and substantiated what until now had been a shot in the dark. His instinct told him he was on the right track.

For the next few minutes, he questioned Thomas at length about Belle Starr. The lawman required little prompting, and gave him an earful regarding the lady bandit's tawdry personal life. Then, moving to a large wall map, Thomas traced the route to Younger's Bend. He allowed it was an easy two day's ride, but cautioned Starbuck to keep his eyes open. The Nations was no place for a man to get careless. And that applied most especially, he added, to a lawman.

Starbuck inquired the best place to buy a horse, and Fagan directed him to a stable on the south side of town. After a few parting remarks, he shook the marshal's hand and thanked him for his assistance. Thomas, waiting near the door, motioned him into the hallway and walked him outside.

On the steps they halted and looked toward the gallows. The death warrant had been read and a minister was intoning a final prayer. Four condemned men stood positioned on the center trap, their hands tied behind their backs and black hoods fitted over their heads. The bearded man Starbuck had seen earlier moved down the line, snugging each noose tight, careful to center the knot below the left ear. Then he turned and walked directly to a wooden lever behind the prisoners. The crowd, morbidly curious, edged closer to the scaffold.

"Who's the hangman?"

"Name's George Maledon," Thomas said stolidly. "Takes pride in his work. Likes to brag he's never let a man strangle to death. Always breaks a fellow's neck first crack out of the box."

"How many men has he hung?"

"That bunch'll make twenty-eight."

A loud *whump* suddenly sounded from the gallows. The four men dropped through the trap door and hit the end of the ropes with an abrupt jolt. Their necks snapped in unison, and their heads, crooked at a grotesque angle, flopped over their right shoulders. The spectators, staring bug-eyed at the scaffold, seemed to hold their breath. Hanging limp, the dead men swayed gently, the scratchy creak of taut rope somehow deafening in the stillness. One eye on his watch, the executioner finally nodded to the prison physician. Working quickly, the doctor moved from body to body, testing for a heartbeat with his stethoscope. A moment later he pronounced the four men officially dead.

Starbuck grunted softly to himself. "Damn shame Judge Parker's not running the whole country."

"How so?"

"Well, from what I've seen, there're more men that deserve hanging than gets hung. Jesse James and his crowd would be prime examples."

"Ain't it a fact!" Thomas paused, then laughed.

"Sure you don't want a job? We could use a man with your style over in the Nations.'

"Thanks all the same." Starbuck turned, his hand outstretched. "I'll stick to Judge Colt. Never have to worry about the verdict that way."

"Hallelujah!" Thomas grinned and pumped his arm with vigor. "Good huntin' to you, Luke."

Starbuck nodded and walked off in the direction of the street. Heck Thomas watched him a moment, wondering on the outcome with Belle Starr and her Cherokee lapdog. Then, as the spectators began dispersing, his attention was drawn to the gallows. The hanged men, one by one, were being unstrung. Somehow, though Thomas wasn't all that superstitious, it seemed prophetic. A favorable sign.

Starbuck ought to have himself a whale of a time at Younger's Bend.

Chapter Six

By late afternoon of the following day Starbuck was some fifty miles west of Fort Smith. The horse he'd bought was a roan gelding with an easy gait and an even disposition. Along with a secondhand saddle and worn range clothes from his warbag, he looked every inch the fiddle-footed cowhand. Which was precisely the role he'd chosen to play at Younger's Bend.

Early on in his career Starbuck had discovered something in himself that went hand in hand with the detective business. He possessed a streak of the actor, and seemed to have a natural flair for disguise. Every assignment differed, and the range of roles he'd played would have challenged a veteran thespian. Over the past few years he had posed as a saddletramp and stockbuyer, con man and grifter, tinhorn gambler and sleazy whoremonger. Experience had taught him that outward appearance fooled most folks most of the time. The balance of the deception required the proper lingo and a working knowledge of the character he portrayed. For that, he had developed the habit of studying other people's quirks of speech and their mannerisms. Operating undercover, his very survival rested on the skill of his performance. So it was he'd honed the trick of transforming himself, both outwardly and inwardly, into someone else. Once he assumed a disguise, he simply ceased to be Luke Starbuck.

For Younger's Bend, he already had a pip of a cover story in mind. All day, riding west from Fort Smith, he'd added a touch here and a touch there. Based on past assignments—the trial and error of mastering his craft—he knew that a credible cover story must always strike a delicate balance. A general rule was the simpler the better, with a guileless, straightforward approach. Yet an element of the outlandish—even something bizarre—added icing to the cake. A happy-go-lucky character who was half fool and half daredevil was the most convincing character of all. Somehow people never suspected a jester whose sights were set on the brass ring. A combination of down-at-the-heels cowhand turned bank robber seemed to Starbuck a real lulu for the task ahead. He thought it would play well at Younger's Bend.

Shortly before sundown Starbuck approached the juncture of the Arkansas and Canadian rivers. Farther west lay the Creek Nation and some distance south lay the Chocktaw Nation. Younger's Bend, which was on the fringe of the Cherokee Nation, was ideally situated to the boundary lines of all three tribes. By rough calculation, he estimated Belle Starr's place was some forty miles upstream along the Canadian. The general direction was southwest, and with no great effort he would arrive there around suppertime tomorrow evening. That fitted perfectly with his plan, for it was essential that he be invited to stop over at least one night. With no reason to travel farther, he decided to pitch camp on the banks of the Arkansas.

A stand of trees was selected for a campsite. There,

with deadwood close to hand, a fire would be no problem. Along with a Winchester carbine he'd bought in Fort Smith, Starbuck dropped his saddlebags and blanket roll at the base of a tree. After being unsaddled, the roan was hobbled and turned loose to graze on a grassy stretch near the riverbank. A fire was kindled, and as dusk fell a cheery blaze lighted the grove.

All in keeping with his role, Starbuck was traveling without camp gear or victuals. He dined on a cold supper of hardtack, store-bought beef jerky, and river water. An hour or so after dark, he picketed the roan between a couple of trees at the edge of the grove. Afterward, with an eye to comfort, he spread his blankets near the fire and covered them with a rain slicker. By then a damp chill had settled over the land, and he decided to call it a night. With his saddle for a pillow, he crawled between the blankets and turned up the collar of his mackinaw. Overhead the indigo sky was clear and flecked through with a zillion stars.

Unable to sleep, he soon tired of counting stars. His thoughts drifted to Younger's Bend, and the reception he might reasonably expect. Then, item by item, he began a mental review of all he'd learned about Belle Starr. With everything contained in the Pinkerton file, added to the rundown by Heck Thomas, it made a hefty package. None of it was good—a sorry account of an even sorrier woman—but revealing all the same. And damned spicy in spots.

Myra Belle Shirley was born in Jasper County, Missouri. Her father, who owned a blacksmith shop and livery stable, was widely respected and prominent in politics. At the proper age, like all proper young ladies, Myra Belle was enrolled in the Carthage Female Academy. There she was taught grammar and deportment, and learned to play a passable tune on the piano. But she was something of a tomboy, and more interested in horses and guns than ladylike refinement. By the time abolitionist Kansas and proslavery Missouri went to war, she was an accomplished horsewoman and no slouch with a pistol.

The border states were savaged during the Civil War, at the mercy of guerrilla bands on both sides. Only fifteen when Quantrill pillaged and burned Lawrence, Kansas, Myra Belle was impressed by the way he had raised a band of volunteers and turned them into a small army of bloodthirsty raiders. Among them was her idol and secret lover, Cole Younger.

In 1863, Myra Belle's older brother was killed when federal troops razed Carthage. Wild with grief she fled home and rode off to join Cole and the guerrillas. For the balance of the war, crazed with revenge, she served as an informant and spy for Quantrill. Then, with the South's surrender, Cole and the James boys took off on their own. She had no choice but to return to her family.

The summer of 1865 Myra Belle's father pulled up roots and moved the family to Texas. Outside Dallas, he bought a farm and dabbled in horse trading. Once more enrolled in school, Myra Belle seemed to have settled down and lost her taste for excitement. Then, early in 1866, Cole Younger rode into the farm with this three brothers and the James boys. Fresh from their first bank robbery, they were flush with money and lavished extravagant gifts on the family. A month or so later, when the gang rode back to Missouri, Cole left an even more lasting memento of the visit. Myra Belle, now a ripe eighteen, was pregnant.

When the child was born out of wedlock, the scandal rocked the farm community. Branded a hussy, Myra Belle left her daughter with her parents and fled to Dallas. There, working as a dance-hall girl, she dropped Myra from her name and became known simply as Belle. There, too, she met and married a young horse thief named Jim Reed. Several years were spent on the run, flitting about from Texas to California, with the law always one step behind. At last, with no place to turn, Reed sought refuge in Indian Territory. Belle shortly joined him, and her career as a lady bandit began in earnest.

The Reeds were given sanctuary by Tom Starr, a full-blood Cherokee. Starr and his eight sons were considered the principal hell-raisers of the Cherokee Nation. Their land was located on a remote stretch of the Canadian River, and considered unsafe for travel by anyone not directly related to the Starr clan. Nonetheless, those who rode the owlhoot were welcome, and even white outlaws found haven there. Belle, the only white woman present, was accorded royal treatment by the Starrs. Then, in the summer of 1874, she abruptly became a widow. Jim Reed, trapped following a stagecoach robbery in Texas, was slain by lawmen.

Never daunted, Belle soon shed her widow's weeds and married Sam Starr. The fact that Sam was a full-blood gave Belle no pause whatever. By the marriage, she gained dower rights to her husband's share in the communal lands of the Cherokee Nation. For the first time in her life she was a woman of property; being white, she was also queen bee of the ruffians who found refuge with the Starr clan. Together she and Sam formed a gang comprising renegade Indians and former cowboys. All were misfits, none of them too bright, and Belle easily dominated the entire crew, her husband included. She promptly dubbed their base of operations Younger's Bend.

The eldest of Old Tom Starr's sons, Sam had a parcel of land located farther downstream on the Canadian. From here, the gang rustled livestock, robbed backwoods stores, and occasionally ran illegal whiskey across the border. Belle was the planner—the brains —and shrewdly brought the men together only when a job was imminent. Afterward, the gang members scattered to Tulsa and other railroad towns to squander their loot. Meanwhile, back at Younger's Bend, Belle and Sam were virtually immune to arrest. Their home was surrounded by wilderness and mountains, and the only known approach was along a canyon trail rising steeply from the river. So inaccessible was the stronghold that lawmen—both Light Horse Police and federal marshals—gave it a wide berth. After ten years in Indian Territory, Belle was riding high and in no great danger of a fall. She was living the life Myra Belle Shirley had sought since girlhood. And she gloried in the notoriety accorded the Nation's one and only lady bandit, Belle Starr.

To Starbuck, it was a challenge with an unusual twist. Yet tonight, warmed by the embers of the fire, he concluded the lady bandit was vulnerable on several counts. Aside from the vanity normal to any woman, there was the added vanity of a woman who had made her mark in a man's world. A woman who ruled her own robbers' roost and considered herself the femme fatale of the James-Younger gang. Such a woman, unless he missed his guess, was likely to have chapped lips from kissing cold mirrors. And a man who played on her vanity might very easily induce her to brag a little. Or maybe a lot, particularly where it concerned an old beau and lingering sentiment. A sentiment expressed in the name itself—Younger's Bend.

Worming deeper into his blankets, Starbuck turned his backsides to the fire. He closed his eyes and drifted toward sleep, thinking of tomorrow. And the lady who was no lady.

In the lowering dusk Starbuck emerged from the canyon trail. Before him, surrounded by dense woods, lay a stretch of level ground. Not fifty yards away, a log house stood like a sentinel where the trail ended. One window was lighted by a lamp.

A flock of crows cawed and took wing as he rode forward. From the house a pack of dogs joined the chorus, and he smiled to himself. On horseback or on foot, there was little chance anyone would approach Younger's Bend unannounced. He noted as well that trees had been felled in a wide swath from the clearing around the house to the mouth of the canyon. The purpose—an unobstructed field of fire—was obvious. He felt a bit like a duck in a shooting gallery.

The door of the house opened and a woman stepped onto the porch. Her features were indistinct, but the lines of her figure and the flow of her dress were silhouetted against lamplight from inside. She hushed the dogs with a sharp command, and stood waiting with her hands on her hips. Starbuck reined to halt in the yard, mindful he wasn't to dismount unless invited. He smiled politely and touched the brim of his hat.

"Evenin', ma'am."

"Evening."

"You'd likely to be Miz Starr."

"Who's asking?"

"Clyde Belden."

"I don't recall we've met, Mr. Belden."

"No, ma'am," Starbuck said briskly. "I was steered to you by a mutual friend."

"Would this friend have a name?"

"Sure does," Starbuck said with the slow whang of a born Missourian. "None other than Jim Younger hisself."

There was the merest beat of hesitation. "Come on inside, Mr. Belden. Just be careful to keep your hands in plain sight."

"Anything you say, Miz Starr."

Starbuck stepped down out of the saddle and left the gelding ground-reined. From the corner of the house, a man materialized out of the shadows. He moved forward, holding a double-barrel shotgun at hip level. In the spill of light from the window, Starbuck immediately pegged him as Sam Starr. He was lithely built, with bark-dark skin, muddy eyes, and sleek, glistening hair. His pinched face had an oxlike expression, and he silently followed along as Starbuck crossed the porch and entered the house. Lagging back, he stopped halfway through the door, the shotgun still leveled.

When Belle Starr turned, Starbuck got the shock of his life. Based on her long string of lovers, he'd expected at the very least a passably attractive woman. Instead, she was horsefaced, with a lantern jaw and bloodless lips and beady close-set eyes. Her figure was somehow mannish, with wide hips and shoulders, and almost no breasts beneath her drab woolen dress. While his expression betrayed nothing, Starbuck thought she looked like a cross between ugly and uglier. He'd seen worse, but only in a circus tentshow.

Inspecting him, Belle's eyes were guarded. He figured the chances of being recognized were slight. It was unlikely the *Police Gazette* had any wide readership in the Nations; only through a fluke would she have seen the issue bearing his photo. Then, too, his face was now covered with bearded stubble, which tended to alter his appearance. At length, watching him closely, she put him to the test.

"What makes you think I know Jim Younger?"

"He told me so!" Starbuck beamed. "Course, I haven't seen him in a spell, but that don't make no nevermind. The day I headed west he told me all about you and Younger's Bend."

"Then you're from Missouri?"

"Born and bred," Starbuck said with cheery vigor. "All us Beldens come from over around Sedalia way."

Belle gave him a veiled but searching look. "I suppose you rode with Jim during the war?"

"No such luck! I got called up and served with the regulars. Jim and me didn't make acquaintance till after the shootin' stopped."

"You mean you rode with him afterwards?"

"Naw," Starbuck said sheepishly. "Jim and me was just drinkin' pals. He used to talk to me about it some, but I didn't have the sand for it in them days."

"So how did he come to mention me?"

"Well, like I said, I decided to cut loose and head

west. Wanted to be a cowboy, and I shore got my wish! Been up the trail from Texas ever' year since the summer of '78."

"You left out the part about Jim."

"Ain't that just like me!" Starbuck rolled his eyes with a foolish smile. "I get started talkin'—well, anyway, Jim told me if I ever got in a tight fix to look you up. So here I am!"

Belle studied him in silence a moment. "What sort of fix?"

"Robbed me a bank!" Starbuck lied heartily. "Walked in all by my lonesome and cleaned 'em out!"

"Where?"

"Vernon," Starbuck informed her. "That's a little burg on the Texas side of the Red River. Figgered it was a good place to get my feet wet."

"Wait a minute." Belle blinked and looked at him. "Are you saying that was your first job?"

"Shore was." Starbuck gave her a lopsided grin. "Pulled it off slicker'n a whistle, too. Got pretty near two thousand in cold cash!"

"Why now?" Belle appeared bemused. "After all this time what changed your mind?"

"Got tired of workin' for thirty a month and found. Thought it over and decided ol' Jim was right. There's easier ways to make a livin', lots easier."

"So what brings you here?"

"By jingo!" Starbuck boomed out jovially. "Where's a better place to lose yourself? The way Jim talked, you're the soul of Christian charity. I just figgered I'd hightail it into the Nations and make your acquaintance. Better late than never!"

Belle seemed to thaw a little. "Clyde, I'd say you've got more sand than you gave yourself credit for."

"Why, thank you, ma'am." Starbuck swept his hat off. "Comin' from you, I take that as a puredee compliment."

"Do you now?" Belle sounded flattered. "What makes you say that?"

"Why, you're famous, Miz Belle! Ole Jimbo thinks the sun rises and sets right where you stand. And it ain't just him either! I've heard Jesse and Cole brag on you till they plumb run out of wind. That's gospel fact!"

"Ooo, go on!" Belle cracked a smile. "I don't believe a word of it."

"Miz Belle, I do admire a modest lady. You make me proud to say I'm an ol' Missouri boy. Yessir, you shorely do!"

From the doorway Sam Starr cleared his throat. Belle glanced in his direction and he jerked his head outside. Then he backed away and turned out of the lamplight spilling through the door. Belle frowned, clearly displeased by her husband's presumptuous manner. After a moment, her gaze shifted to Starbuck and she smiled.

"Have a seat." She waved him to a crude dining table. "I'll be with you in a minute."

"Thank you kindly." Starbuck took a chair and tossed his hat on the table. "Don't rush on my account, Miz Belle. I got time to spare."

Belle merely nodded and walked swiftly from the room. Outside, she wheeled right and strode to the end of the porch. Sam was stationed where he could watch the door, the shotgun cradled over one arm. His view through the window was partially obstructed by the angle, but he could see the edge of the dining table and Starbuck's hat. Belle stopped, fixing him with an annoyed squint. Her voice was harsh, cutting.

"What the fuck's your problem?"

"Not me," Sam grunted coarsely. "That feller in there's the problem."

"If you've got something to say, why don't you just spit it out?"

"You ain't gonna like it."

"Try me and see."

"We got to kill him, Belle. Kill him now!"

Chapter Seven

Starbuck sat stock-still. He listened as Belle's footsteps rapidly crossed the porch, then there was silence. His smile vanished and his eyes flicked around the room.

The interior of the house was smaller than it appeared from outside. Stoutly built, with chinked log walls, it consisted of a central living area and a separate bedroom. The battered table and chairs stood before an open fireplace with a mud chimney. A commode with a faded mirror occupied the wall beside the bedroom door. An ancient brass bed, visible through the door, gleamed in the flames from the fireplace. To the rear of the main room was a wood cooking stove and rough-hewn shelves packed with canned goods. A jumble of odds and ends was piled in the far corner.

On the whole, it was sparse on comfort and smelled like a wolf den. Yet Starbuck wasn't concerned with tidiness or the accommodations. He was looking for a back door—all too aware his Colt was no match for a shotgun at close quarters, and suddenly uncomfortable that the only exit was the door through which he had entered. His attention turned to the powwow under way on the front porch. There was no question he was the topic of conversation, but considerable doubt existed as to the verdict. He subscribed to the theory of shoot first and talk about it later, and a vantage point nearer the door seemed eminently advisable. Then, too, a bit of eavesdropping might very well improve his odds.

Quietly, Starbuck rose and moved to the fireplace. He stood with his hands outstretched to the flames, one eye on the window. No one was watching him—nor was there any sound from outside—and he concluded they were still huddled at the end of the porch. Hugging the wall, he ghosted toward the front of the house. There, he flattened himself beside the windowsill and pressed his ear to the logs. The chinking was old and cracked, seeping air between small gaps, and through it he heard the drone of voices. A heated argument was under way.

"I don't give a good goddamn what you think!"

"You'd better," Sam grumbled. "I got a nose for those things."

"Heap big Injun!" Belle mocked him. "You'd starve to death if somebody hadn't invented tinned goods!"

"You got no call to say that."

"Oh, no? When's the last time you and your mangy pack of brothers shot a deer—or a rabbit—or even a squirrel, for Chrissakes? You've got a hunter's nose like I've got warts on my ass!"

"I'm warnin' you now! You leave my brothers outta this!"

"Awww, dry up," Belle said in a waspish tone. "The whole bunch of you couldn't hold a candle to a cigar-store Indian. Your pa's the only one with any balls—and it sure as hell didn't get passed along to you!"

"How come you're always throwin' the old man up in my face?"

"Because nobody ever pulled his tail feathers. Go on, admit it! You're full-grown and you still wet your pants anytime he looks cross-eyed at you."

"Mebbe you should've married him 'stead of me."

"Maybe!" Belle crowed. "Jesus Christ, no maybe about it! At least he's still got some red-hot Injun blood left in him. Which is more than I can say for you and your butthole brothers."

Sam laughed without mirth. "Won't work, Belle! I ain't gonna get mad."

"Talk sense! What the Sam Hill's that got to do with anything?"

"'Cause you're tryin' to throw me off the scent and we both know it."

"Here we go again," Belle gibed. "You and your track-'em-through-the-woods nose!"

"I know a lawdog when I smell one."

"Sam, you poor sap! You couldn't smell a fart if somebody caught it in a bottle and let you have the first sniff."

"I am warnin' you, woman. That feller's no bank robber! I'll betcha he don't know Jim Younger nor none of the others either."

"Judas Priest," Belle groaned. "You heard me question him! You were standing there the whole time and I didn't trip him up once. How do you explain that?"

"I didn't say he was dumb," Sam reminded her. "I said he was a lawdog! So it just naturally figgers he'd have all the right answers. Any fool oughta see that."

"Are you calling me a fool, Sam Starr?"

"No, I ain't. I'm only tryin' to talk some sense into your head."

"Well, you can talk till you're blue in the face and it won't change a thing. I told you once and I'm telling you again! I won't let you kill him."

"Too bad your brains ain't where they're supposed to be."

"What the hell does that mean?"

"It means you've got hot drawers, that's what it means."

"You're crazy as a loon!"

"Yeah?" Sam bristled. "You think I don't know the sign when I see it? You got your mind set on him humpin' you, and you ain't gonna listen to reason till he forks you good and proper."

"That's a dirty goddamn lie!"

"Belle, how many men you humped since we got married? Mebbe you lost count, but I haven't. I watched it happen enough times I know what I'm talkin' about. You don't want me to kill him 'cause you got hot drawers. So don't tell me different."

"Well, so what?" Belle lashed out. "I go to bed with any damn body I please. I don't need your permission!"

"Never said otherwise," Sam conceded. "All I'm sayin' is, we'd be better off with him dead. So I'll wait till after you're done and then kill him. How's that?"

"No deal," Belle said sternly. "I will budge a little, though. We'll let him spend the night and then send him on his way. Fair enough?"

"I wisht you'd believe me when I tell you he's a lawman. Probably sent personal by the Hangin' Judge hisself."

"You think I don't know a Missouri boy when I see one? He's no more a marshal than you are. Hell's bells, I'm a better judge of character than that!"

"So go on and suit yourself. You always do anyway."

"Sam?"

"Yeah?"

"Don't get any wiseass notions about killing him after he leaves here. You do and I'll wait till you're asleep some night—and then I'll cut your goddamn tallywhacker clean off! You hear me, Sam?"

"I hear you."

Starbuck heard her, too. He was again seated at the dining table when Belle led her husband through the door. Several things were apparent to him from their conversation. Foremost was that he would have only one night to squeeze Belle dry of information. Another factor, which might serve to loosen her tongue, was that she'd bought his story about Jim Younger. Yet, like an alley cat in heat, she had designs on his body, and big plans for the night ahead. One look at her gargoyle face and he began having second thoughts about the detective business. He wasn't sure he could get it up—much less romance her—even in the cause of law and order.

Sam halted near the door and Belle moved directly to the table. Watching her, Starbuck wondered how it would work with a sack over her head. He thought it an idea worth exploring.

"Forgot to introduce you boys," Belle said, gesturing toward the door. "Clyde, want you to meet my husband—Sam Starr."

"Howdy, Sam." Starbuck nodded amiably. "Pleasure's all mine."

Sam muttered something unintelligible, and Belle quickly resumed. "How would you like to stay to supper and spend the night?"

"Why, I'd be most obliged, Miz Belle."

"We'd ask you to stay longer, but it wouldn't work out just now. We've got a business deal of our own that won't keep."

"No problem," Starbuck said agreeably. "I was just passin' through, anyhow. Only stopped off to pay my respects."

"Too bad in a way." Belle feigned a rueful look. "You and Sam would probably get a kick out of chewing the fat. But he's got to run over to his pa's place and tend to that business deal. Don't you, Sam?"

"Yeah, sure." Sam gave her a disgruntled scowl, then turned toward the door. "See you in the mornin'."

A few minutes later, Belle watched from the porch while her husband led a horse from the barn and mounted. When the hoofbeats faded into the night, she stepped back inside and closed the door. She smiled like a tigress stalking a goat.

Starbuck, cast in the role of the goat, had a sudden sinking feeling. It looked to be a long night.

Whatever else she was, Belle Starr was no cook. She served Starbuck sowbelly and beans, a pasty hominy gruel, and cornbread baked hard as sandstone. He wolfed it down with gusto—grinning all the while—and topped off the performance with an appreciative belch. The belch was the easiest part, and required no strain. He felt gassy as a bloated hog.

After clearing the table, Belle brought out a couple of tin cups and a quart of rotgut. The whiskey had a bite like molten lead, and tasted as though it had been aged in a turpentine barrel. No sipper, Belle was clearly a lady who enjoyed her liquor. She poured with the regularity of a metronome, and slugged it down without batting an eye. Starbuck, sensing opportunity, matched her shot for shot. She wanted his body and he wanted information, and it all boiled down to who got crocked first. Unless she had a hollow leg, he thought there was a reasonable chance he could outlast her.

In passing, Starbuck noted that he'd been dead on the mark regarding her vanity. She was a woman with a high opinion of herself, and not above putting on airs. Earlier, on the porch with Sam, she had displayed the foul mouth of a veteran muleskinner. Yet with Starbuck, her language bordered on the ladylike, sweeter than sugar and twice as nice. The more she drank, the more he had to admire her style. For a virtuoso of four-letter words, it took considerable restraint to hobble her tongue. He mentally applauded the effort, and bided his time waiting for her to slip back into character. Only then would he make his move.

Along toward midnight, Starbuck's patience was rewarded. The bottle of popskull was approaching empty, and Belle's eyes were fixed in a glassy stare that seemed vaguely out of focus. She wasn't ossified, but her tolerance to snakebite would last well into next week. Starbuck was feeling a little numb himself, warmed by a tingling sensation that extended to his hair roots. Yet he still had his wits about him, and it appeared he'd won the drinking bout. The lady bandit suddenly reverted to her true self. And her choice of words was all the tipoff he needed.

"You know something, Clyde?" Her mouth curled in a coy smile. "For an old Missouri boy, you're a goddamn sweet-looking man."

"Well, Miz Belle"—Starbuck grinned, suppressing his revulsion, and plunged ahead—"you're pretty easy on the eyes yourself."

"Forget that Miz Belle shit. I'm not your mama and you're not wet behind the ears. You follow me?"

Starbuck's grin turned to a suggestive leer. "What'd you have in mind?"

"When I was a girl—" Belle burst out in a bawdy horselaugh. "All the prissy-assed little buttermouths at the Female Academy called it the birds and the bees. Once I took up with boys, I learned it was better known as stink finger and hide the weenie. That answer your question?"

"Sounds the least bit like an invitation."

"I never was one to mince words. A woman's got the same needs as a man."

"Some folks call it horny."

"By God, Clyde, you're a card! Always was partial to a man with a sense of humor."

"What about Sam?" Starbuck jerked his chin at the door. "I'd hate to have him come bustin' in here with that shotgun just when I was all set to flush the birds out of your nest."

"Wooiee!" Belle leaned forward, grabbing his head in both hands, and planted one smack on his lips. "Flush the birds out of my nest! Goddamn, that's rich, Clyde. I do like the sound of it!"

Starbuck felt like he'd been kissed by a dragon. "Not to put a damper on things, but I'd shore like to hear your answer about Sam."

"Who gives a fuck?" Belle gave him a sly and tipsy look. "I sent Sam packing for the night, and that's that! You just rest easy, sport."

Starbuck paused, then smoothly laid the trap. "Well, now, I dunno. Jim told me about you and Cole, but I just naturally figgered—"

"What about Cole?"

"Why, that you was sweet on him. The way Jim talked it went back long before the war."

Belle poured herself a stiff shot and knocked it back. "What else did he tell you?"

"Say, look here—" Starbuck broke off with a troubled frown. "I don't want to step on nobody's toes. Maybe I'd best let it drop there."

"No, you don't!" Belle demanded. "You started it, now finish it!"

"Listen, Belle, me and Jim go way back. I shore wouldn't wanna get him in dutch."

"Oh, for God's sake!" Belle drunkenly waved the objection aside. "I won't hold it against Jim. Now stop dancing around and spill it! What'd he tell you?"

"Nothin' much, really." Starbuck's tone was matter-of-fact. "Only that you let Cole and the boys hide out here after they'd pulled a job. I seem to recollect he mentioned Jesse and Frank, too."

The effects of her last drink suddenly overtook Belle. She squinted owlishly and her speech slurred. "How about Ruston's place?"

Starbuck held his breath. "You mean the other hideout?"

"Yeah."

"Wait a minute!" Starbuck wrinkled his brow in concentration. "Why, shore, Ruston! Near as I recall, Jim said he'd served with 'im under Quantrill. Now what the blue-billy-hell was his first name? Got it right on the tip of my tongue!"

"Tom," Belle mumbled. "Good ol' Tom Ruston. Wish I had his spread and he had a feather up his ass! We'd both be tickled pink."

Starbuck played along. "Jim said it was some layout."

"One of the biggest." Belle nodded. "And on the Pecos, that's saying a lot! Nothing smalltime about Texans."

"You're tellin' me!" Starbuck laughed. "I reckon I've trailed enough cows outta Texas to have a pretty fair idee." He hesitated, choosing his words. "Well, maybe I'll run acrost Jim down there one of these days."

"Not likely." Belle sloshed whiskey into her cup, wholly unaware she had emptied the bottle. "Long as they're safe here, they got no reason to bother Ruston."

Starbuck decided not to press it further. The last piece of the puzzle was now clear, and all that remained was to fit the parts together. With a broad grin, he lifted his cup in a toast. "Here's to the Youngers! Ol' King Cole and the best damn brothers any man could ask for."

"I'll drink to that!"

Belle drained her cup in a long swallow and lowered it to her lap. Whiskey dribbled down her chin and she burped, clapping her hand to her mouth with a foolish giggle. She gave Starbuck a dopey smile and reached for his hand. Then a wave of dizziness rocked her, and her eyes suddenly glazed. The cup clattered to the floor and her head thumped forward onto the table.

Starbuck lifted her from her chair and carried her to the bedroom. She was out cold and lay like a corpse while he undressed her. Unmoved by her nakedness, he pulled the covers up to her chin and turned away. At the door, he glanced back and let go a heavy sigh of relief.

He felt like a condemned man with a last-minute reprieve.

Late the next morning Starbuck led his horse from the barn and halted before the house. Belle, suffering from a monumental hangover, stood on the porch. He gave her a lewd wink and playfully patted her on the thigh.

"You're some woman, Miz Belle Starr. One of a kind!"

Belle's eyes were bloodshot, vaguely disoriented. "Clyde, tell me something. How'd things work out last night?"

"You don't remember?"

"Not just exactly. Did you—uh—flush the birds out of the nest?"

"Did I ever!" Starbuck whooped. "Scattered 'em all to hell and gone!"

"Yeah?" Belle seemed bemused. "Well, how was it?"

"Never had none better! You plumb tuckered me out, and that's the gospel truth."

Belle brightened visibly. "You Missouri boys always was hot-blooded."

"Godalmightybingo! Stink finger and hide the weenie! Wouldn't have missed it for the world, Miz Belle!"

Starbuck tossed her a roguish salute and stepped into the saddle. He turned the gelding out of the yard and gigged him into a prancing trot. At the mouth of the canyon, he twisted around and waved his hat high overhead. Belle, looking fluttery as a school girl, threw him a kiss.

The performance ended as Starbuck rode toward the river. His jaw hardened and his mouth set in a tight line. For the moment, Indian Territory was a washout, and he saw nothing to be gained in scouting the ranch on the Pecos. All of which meant he'd exhausted his options. Jesse James would have to be hunted down on homeground.

He forded the river and headed north, toward Missouri. And Clay County.

Chapter Eight

A cold blue dusk settled over the winter landscape.

Lamar Hudspeth waited in the shadows of the barn. With his son at his side, he watched three riders approach along the rutted wagon road. A snowfall, followed by a brief warm spell, had turned the road into a boggy quagmire. The horses slogged through the mud, heads bowed against a brisk wind, snorting frosty clouds of vapor. Their riders reined off the road and proceeded toward the barn at a plodding walk. Hudspeth stepped out of the shadows.

"Cole." He greeted the men by name as they dismounted. "Jim, you're lookin' fit. Evenin', Bob."

"How do, Lamar."

Cole Younger merely bobbed his head. "Jesse here yet?"

"Nope," Hudspeth replied with a shrug. "He'll be along directly though. Probably waitin' till it gets full dark."

"Horseshit!" Cole loosed a satiric laugh. "He's

waitin' to see if we get ourselves ambushed. Jesse always was good at lettin' somebody else bird-dog for him."

"You got no call to talk that way, Cole."

"Think not? Then how come we're the first ones here when it's him that called the meetin'? Go on, answer me that!"

"I 'spect he's got his reasons."

"Lamar, there's none your equal when it comes to stickin' by kinfolk. I'll hand you that."

"Speakin' of kin," Hudspeth said, easing into another subject, "I made the rounds today. Stopped by Miz Samuel's place, just to make sure there wasn't no outsiders nosin' about."

"We done the same," Cole remarked, motioning to his brothers. "All of us snuck in to see our women last night. Things appear to be pretty quiet."

"So Miz Samuel said," Hudspeth acknowledged. "She ain't seen hide nor hair of anybody that looks like a Pinkerton."

"Jesse's wife still stayin' with his ma?"

"Well, her being in a family way and all, I 'spect she'll stay there till her time comes."

"Leastways Jesse don't need no bird dog there. One way or another, he manages to sire his own pups."

"Iffen it was me, I wouldn't let Jesse hear you say a thing like that."

"Before the night's over, he's gonna hear lots worse. I got a bellyful, and I aim to speak my piece."

"I reckon you're full-growed." Hudspeth gestured to his son. "The boy'll put your horses in the barn. There's coffee on the stove and angel cake for them that wants it."

"Your woman's braver'n most, Lamar."

"How's that?"

"Bakin' an angel cake for this crew? Damnation, she's liable to get your house struck by lightning!"

Cole laughed and walked off with his brothers. The

Hudspeth boy, flushed with shame for his father, led their horses into the barn. For his part, Lamar Hudspeth took no offense at the crude humor. His one concern was that there would be no spillover of animosity tonight. Yet, from all indications, he sensed that it wasn't to be. Cole Younger was plainly looking for an excuse to start trouble.

The Hudspeth farm was located some miles outside the town of Kearney. Hudspeth himself was a law-abiding family man, a deacon in the Baptist church, and modestly active in Clay County politics. He was also a second cousin of Jesse and Frank James. Though he abhorred their methods—for he was a fundamentalist who took the Scriptures literally—he nonetheless believed they were being persecuted by shylock bankers and unscrupulous railroad barons. Like many people, he assisted the James boys and the Youngers at every turn. Since their own homes were unsafe, the gang members found shelter with friends and relatives; constantly on the move, they seldom spent more than a couple of nights in any one spot. The system baffled the law and allowed the robbers to visit their wives and children on a sporadic basis.

After nearly seventeen years, the people of Clay County had grown accustomed to a climate of conspiracy and distrust. Their efforts on behalf of the gang were now commonplace, an everyday part of life. Not unlike measles or whooping cough, it was accepted as the natural order of things.

Lamar Hudspeth, no different from his neighbors, would have scoffed at the notion that he was aiding and abetting outlaws. The James boys were kinsmen, and the Youngers, with the possible exception of Cole, were old and valued friends. Honor dictated that he shield them from harm and forever take their part in the struggle against the Pinkertons. Tonight, as he had on past occasions, he had consented to let them meet in his home. He recognized the danger and gave it no more than passing consideration. They were, after all, family.

A short while after dark Jesse and Frank emerged from the woods north of the house. Hudspeth wasn't surprised, and while he'd denied it earlier, he knew Cole Younger was right all along. Jesse was a cautious man, forever leery of a trap; it was no accident he hadn't arrived on time for the meeting. Instead, waiting in the trees, he had probably watched the house since well before dusk. Hudspeth thought it a sensible precaution, if not altogether admirable. Yet there was no condemnation in the thought. He never judged a kinsman.

Jesse reined to a halt and swung down out of the saddle. He was lean, with stark features and a cleft chin and cold slate-colored eyes. His beard was neatly trimmed, and he carried himself with the austere, straight-backed posture that bordered on arrogance. He was a man of dour moods and he seldom smiled. His natural expression was rocklike, wholly devoid of sentiment.

By contrast, Frank was courteous and thoughtful, with a warm smile and an affable manner. Quietly studious, he was self-educated and an ardent reader, especially partial to the works of Shakespeare. To the dismay of the other gang members, he liberally quoted the Bard whenever the occasion permitted. Among friends and family, it was an open secret that he supplied the wording for Jesse's articulate letters to the newspaper editors. Except for the dominance of his brother, he might have been a scholar, or a man of the cloth. He was, instead, an outlaw with a price on his head.

After a round of handshakes, Jesse cut his eyes toward the house. "Cole and the boys inside?"

Hudspeth nodded. "Cole's some put out 'cause you wasn't here first. Hope there won't be any trouble."

"Cole's all wind and no whistle. He just likes to hear himself talk."

"Maybe so," Hudspeth said, without conviction. "He's on a tear tonight, though. Told me he'd had a bellyful and meant to get it out in the open."

"Bellyful of what?"

"Search me," Hudspeth responded. "I just listen, Jesse. I don't meddle."

"One of these days," Jesse said crossly, "I'm gonna fix his little red wagon for good."

"C'mon now, Jess," Frank gently admonished. "Cole doesn't mean any harm. He just flies off the handle every now and then, that's all. Besides, it wouldn't do to forget . . . you need him and the boys."

The men stood for a moment in a cone of silence. Then, to no one in particular, Hudspeth spoke. "Saw your ma today."

"Figured you might." Jesse's expression mellowed slightly. "She all right?"

"Tolerable," Hudspeth allowed. "Got herself a touch of rheumatism, and that's slowed her up some. Course, she ain't one to complain."

"No, it's not her way. How's Zee?"

Hudspeth looked down and studied the ground. "She asked me to pass along a message."

"Yeah?"

"She ain't happy with your ma, Jesse. One woman under another woman's roof puts a strain on everybody concerned. She asked me to tell you she wants a place of her own."

Jesse acted as though he hadn't heard. "Well," he said, after a measurable pause, "I guess we'd best get the meeting started. What with one thing and another, it's liable to take awhile."

Hudspeth pursed his lips, on the verge of saying something more. Then, reluctant to meddle, his gaze shifted to Frank. "Sorry I didn't get by to see Annie. Between chores and all, there just wasn't time enough."

"In our line of work," Frank said with a rueful smile, "wives learn to take catch as catch can. All the same, I'm planning to slip into home tonight when we're done here. I'll tell her you asked after her."

"Let's get on with it." Jesse started off, then turned back. "Lamar, you aim to keep a lookout while we're inside?"

"No need to fret," Hudspeth assured him. "Anybody comes along, I'll send the boy to fetch you lickety-split."

"What about Sarah?"

"She knows to stay in the kitchen. If you'll recollect, she never wanted to hear nothin' about your business anyhow."

With a querulous grunt, Jesse trudged off in the direction of the house. Frank traded glances with Hudspeth, then tagged along on his brother's heels. Upon entering the house, they found the Youngers seated around the parlor. Bob and Jim greeted them civilly enough, but Cole opted for brooding silence. An air of tension seemed to permeate the room.

No one spoke as Jesse hung his coat and hat on a wall peg beside the entrance. Without a word, he crossed the parlor and closed a door leading to the kitchen. Frank, fearing the worst, lowered himself into a rocker and began stuffing his pipe. Then, once more crossing the room, Jesse took a chair directly across from Cole. His eyes were metallic.

"I understand you've got your bowels in an uproar?"

"You understand right."

"Then spit it out, and be damn quick about it!"

Cole reddened, stung by his tone. An oak of a man, with brutish features and a square jaw, the eldest of the Younger brothers was ruled by a volatile temper. Yet, where Jesse was concerned, his outbursts were generally of short duration. For years he had allowed himself to be intimidated by the gang leader's autocratic manner. His deference, though he had never admitted it to anyone, was due in no small part to fear. He knew Jesse would kill without pretext or provocation, the way a fox mindlessly slaughters a coop full of chickens. Tonight, however, he was determined to stand his ground. His jaw set in a bulldog scowl, and his gaze was steady.

"Me and the boys"—he motioned to his brothers—"are fed up! We want a bigger say in how this outfit's run. All the more so since you likely called us together to plan a job."

Jesse nailed him with a corrosive stare. "Suppose we leave Bob and Jim out of it. You're the one that's got a hair across his ass! So let's just keep it between ourselves."

"That ain't so," Cole corrected him. "We talked it out and we're of a mind. We've got to have more say so in how things are done."

"Don't make me laugh." Jesse's voice was alive with contempt. "The three of you together don't have brains enough to pour piss out of a boot. Without me to do your thinking for you, you'd starve to death in nothing flat."

"Bullfeathers!" Cole said defiantly. "We ain't been doing so *hot with* you! Our last couple of jobs was nickel-and-dime stuff. Keep on that way and we'll have to take up honest work to make a livin'."

"Quit bellyaching! You and the boys have done all right for yourselves."

"No, we ain't neither! You bollixed our last bank job and that train holdup last summer was a regular gawddamn disaster. All we done was kill a lot of people! And in case it slipped your mind, that ain't exactly the purpose in pullin' a robbery."

An evil light began to dance in Jesse's eyes. He glanced at Bob and Jim, and they seemed to cower before the menace in his gaze. Neither of them spoke, and their hangdog expressions evidenced little support for their brother. At length, Jesse swung back to Cole.

"Sounds like you've got some idea of moving me aside and stepping into my boots."

"Never said that," Cole protested. "All I'm sayin' is that we want a vote in the way things are handled."

"A vote!" Jesse fixed him with a baleful look. "We don't operate by ballot. Only one man around here calls the shots—and that's me!"

"Confound it, Jesse!" Cole said explosively. "That won't cut the ice no more. We're done takin' orders like we was a bunch of ninnies! Either you treat us square or else—"

"Don't threaten me." Jesse's tone was icy. "You do, and I'm liable to forget your name's Younger."

"Whoa back now!" Frank struck into the argument with a gentle rebuke. "You two keep on that way and we'll all wind up losers. Jesse, it wouldn't hurt anything to listen. Why not let Cole have his say?"

"Are you taking sides against me?"

Frank appraised his brother with a shrewd glance. "You ought to know better than to even ask such a thing. I'm just trying to get you to listen, that's all. We have to divvy up the same bone—so where's the harm?"

"Well . . ." Jesse said doubtfully. "I don't mind listening. I just don't want anybody telling me I don't know my business."

"Never said that either," Cole insisted. "But Frank hit the nail on the head. We ain't had a decent payday in a long gawddamn time, and it wouldn't hurt to take a new slant on things."

"A new slant?" Jesse repeated stiffly. "What's that supposed to mean?"

"For one thing," Cole explained, "we've got to give a little more thought to the Pinkertons. The way I see it, they pretty well got us euchred."

"Awww, for God's sake," Jesse said with heavy sarcasm. "You're crazy as a hoot owl! How long's it been since a Pinkerton set foot in Clay County?"

"Fat lotta good that does us! They've figured out we only operate in certain states and they've got everybody nervy as a cat in a roomful of rockers. We haven't hit one bank or one train in the last year that wasn't halfway expectin' to be robbed."

"So what's your idea? Should we start robbing poor boxes, candy stores—what?"

"No," Cole said with an unpleasant grunt. "I think we ought to consider explorin' new territory."

"Don't tell me," Jesse taunted him. "Let me guess. You've got just the place picked out—am I right?"

"Now that you mention it," Cole noted with vinegary satisfaction, "I stumbled across a real humdinger. A friend had some kinfolk move up there, and the way their letters read, the streets are paved with gold."

"Up where?"

"Minnesota," Cole informed him. "Northfield, Minnesota."

"You are nuts!" Jesse snorted. "What the hell's in Minnesota worth robbing?"

"A bank," Cole replied in a sandy voice. "I had my friend write his relatives—all nice and casual—and it turns out Northfield's smack-dab in the center of things up that way. And there's only *one* bank. A big bank!"

"There's lots of big banks, and lots closer, too. Hell's fire, Minnesota must be three hundred miles away, maybe more."

"I checked," Cole said without expression. "Northfield's right at four hundred miles from where we're sittin'."

"That corks it!" Jesse said, almost shouting. "Why in Christ's name would we ride four hundred miles to rob a bank?"

"Because it's the last place on earth the Pinkertons would expect us to hit. So far as I'm concerned, that's about the best reason there is. You stop and think on it, and you'll see I'm right."

A thick silence settled over the room. Jesse caught Frank's eye, and they exchanged a long, searching stare. Then, with a somber look, Frank slowly bobbed his head.

"It makes sense, Jess. I never heard of Northfield, and I doubt that the Pinkertons have either. Matter of fact, it's so far out of our usual territory, they'd probably blame the job on someone else."

Jesse heaved himself to his feet. He began to pace around the parlor, hands stuffed in his pockets. No one spoke, and the tread of his footsteps seemed somehow oppressive in the stillness. After a time, he stopped, his head bowed, studying the floor. At last, as though to underline the question, he raised his head and looked Frank squarely in the eye.

"Are you voting with Cole?"

"Jess—" Frank paused, weighing his words. "I couldn't vote one way or the other, not till we've got more details. I'm only saying the idea itself sounds good."

"All right," Jesse said in a resigned voice. "Here's the way we'll work it. Since Bob's the best scout we've got, he goes to Northfield to check the layout. I want to know everything there is to know about the bank and the town. And most especially, I want you to map out a step-by-step escape route to Belle Starr's place. You got that straight, Bob?"

"Sure do, Jesse." Bob grinned, sitting erect in his chair. "I'll leave first thing in the mornin'."

Jesse considered a moment. "I figure two weeks ought to do it. That'll push you a little, but not too bad. So unless I send word to the contrary, we'll all meet back here two weeks from tonight. Any questions?"

There were no questions. Jesse looked around the room, and his eyes were suddenly stern, commanding. "One last thing. Lay low and stay out of trouble. We don't want to draw attention to ourselves just before we pull a job." He paused, and added a blunt afterthought. "Cole, that goes for you more than the others. None of your monkeyshines down at Ma Ferguson's."

Cole darted a glance at Frank, then shrugged. "No nookie for two weeks? That's a pretty tall order."

"Tie a string on it and keep it in your pants."

"We ain't all got your will power, Jesse."

"You've argued with me enough for one night. Just do like I say."

"Well, I'll give 'er a try. Yessir, I shore will!"

Jesse stared at him a moment. Then, nodding to Frank, he turned toward the door. With no word of parting, he shrugged into his coat and stepped into the night. Frank, trading one last look with Cole, dutifully tagged along.

The parlor suddenly seemed ominously quiet.

Chapter Nine

Starbuck rode into Clay County on a bleak February evening. The sky was heavy with clouds and beneath it the frozen trees swayed in a polar wind. His destination was Ma Ferguson's roadhouse.

Upon returning from Indian Territory, he had laid over several days in Kansas City. The delay, though it had grated on him, was unavoidable. He'd needed time to perfect a disguise, and assume yet another identity. There was every reason to believe that the *Police Gazette*—which frequently carried articles about the James-Younger gang—was widely read in Clay County. His photo, which had appeared in the same publication, would have proved a dead giveaway. The upshot, were he to be recognized, was none too pleasant to contemplate. He wisely undertook a transformation in his appearance.

A theatrical supplier was his first stop. Kansas City was a crossroads for show companies, and the supplier stocked all manner of props and costumes. There, Starbuck obtained a bottle of professional hair dye, choosing dark nut-brown as a suitable contrast to his light chestnut mane. The proprietor assured him a dye job would last several weeks, barring a hard rain or any great penchant for hot baths. As an added touch, Starbuck also bought a spit-curled mustache of the same color. Though fake, the mustache was quality work; even on close examintion it looked to be the genuine article. A liberal application of spirit gum guaranteed it would remain glued to his upper lip.

While arranging the disguise, Starbuck had re-viewed his mental catalogue on Clay County. From the Pinkerton file, he recalled that the Younger brothers were notorious womanizers. The James boys, for all their quickness with a gun, were faithful husbands and devoted family men. But the Youngers, par-ticularly Cole, were known to frequent a brothel operated by one Ma Ferguson. Located outside the town of Liberty, the bawdyhouse was situated in the southwestern tip of the county, and apparently ca-tered to the rougher element. Somewhat remote, lying on a backcountry road between Kearney and Liberty, it was a place to be avoided by strangers. According to the Pinkerton file, it was considered a certain-death assignment for both law officers and private investigators. No undercover operative had ever at-tempted to infiltrate Ma Ferguson's cathouse.

Starbuck thought it the most likely place to start. For one thing, he would arouse less suspicion simply because the Pinkertons, for the last eight years, had steered clear of the dive. For another, it would allow him to observe the gang—perhaps strike up an ac-quaintance—when they were most vulnerable. Men intent on swilling booze and rutting with whores were almost certain to lower their guard. Then, too, the easygoing atmosphere of a brothel fitted nicely with his overall plan. Ma Ferguson's was but an initial step, a matter of establishing himself and gaining the con-fidence of the girls who worked there. His ultimate goal was to infiltrate the James-Younger gang itself.

Starbuck had devised a cock-and-bull story that was entirely plausible. He would pose as a horse thief— operating out of Dodge City—who was now on the run from Kansas lawmen. Dodge City, billing itself as the Queen of Cowtowns, was also the current horse-flesh capital of the West. Along with the longhorn herds driven to railhead, thousands of horses were trailed up each year from Texas. Some were sold there; others were moved north, to distant markets in Montana and Wyoming. Horse thieves, like wolves sniffing fresh scent, had made Dodge City their head-quarters. And therein lay his cover story. One thief, forced to take the owlhoot, would draw little in the way of curiosity. It was an occupational hazard, all part of the game. So common, in fact, that wanted posters were no longer circulated on horse thieves.

All that remained was to attract the attention of the Younger brothers. A high roller, throwing his money to the winds, would do for openers. Then, somewhere along the line, he would find a way to impress them, and gain their favor. Only then would they accept him as a thief who aspired to greater things, one who deserved their consideration. And only then, when he'd wormed his way into their ranks, would he get the chance he sought. A shot at Jesse James.

The plan entailed a high degree of risk. One slip— the slightest miscue—and he was a dead man. Yet, at the same time, his charade would represent the safest possible approach. The Youngers would never suspect that a private detective, alone and unaided, would invade their favorite whorehouse. Nor would they guess that his audacity was less invention than necessity. Try as he might, he'd thought of nothing else that would work in Clay County.

Shortly after nightfall, Starbuck rode into the yard of Ma Ferguson's place. The house was a large two-story structure, brightly lighted and painted a dazzling white. He thought the color an ironic choice—one sel-dom associated with ladies of negotiable virtue—and instantly pegged Ma Ferguson for a woman with a sense of humor. Stepping down from the saddle, he loosened the cinch and left the roan tied to a hitch rack out front. Then, dusting himself off, he strode boldly into the house.

The front room, as in most bordellos, was fashioned on the order of a parlor. Sofas and chairs were scattered at random, with a small bar in one corner and an upright piano along the far wall. The hour was still early, and only two customers, townsmen by their dress, were in evidence. The girls, nearly a dozen in number, lounged on the sofas while a black man with pearly teeth pounded out a tune on the piano. Ma Ferguson, a large, heavyset woman in her forties, was seated in an overstuffed armchair. She gave Starbuck's range clothes a slow once-over, then smiled and waved him to the bar.

"First one's on the house, dearie!"

"Thank you, ma'am." Starbuck doffed his Stetson and hooked it on a hatrack. "Don't mind if I do."

Walking forward, he halted at the bar and ordered rye. Before the barkeep finished pouring, a girl appeared at his elbow. Her eyelids were darkned with kohl and her cheeks were bright with rouge. She smiled a bee-stung smile.

"Hello there, handsome."

"Hello yourself." Starbuck gave her a burlesque leer. "Buy you a drink?"

"My mama taught me to never say no."

Starbuck laughed, his face wreathed in high good humor. "I shore hope that don't apply just to drinks."

"Why, honeybunch, you can bet your boots on it!"

The girl was a pocket Venus. She was small and saucy, with a gamine quality that was compellingly attractive. Her delicate features were framed by ash-blond hair, and her wraparound housecoat fitted snugly across fruity breasts and tightly rounded buttocks. She fixed him with a smile that would have melted the heart of a drill sergeant.

"Let me guess." Her eyes sparkled with suppressed mirth. "You're a cowboy, aren't you?"

"Close," Starbuck said with a waggish grin. "You might say I'm a horsetrader."

"Nooo," she breathed. "Really?"

"Sometimes." Starbuck's grin broadened. "Course, it all depends."

"On what?"

"On whose horses we're tradin'."

She threw back her head and laughed. "Sweetie, I do like a man who likes a joke!"

"Well, little lady, I've got a hunch your gonna like me lots."

"I'm Alvina." She leaned closer, squashing a breast against his arm. "What's your name . . . horse trader?"

"Floyd Hunnewell." Starbuck cocked one eye askew. "Fresh from Kansas and hot to trot."

"Then you've come to the right place, Floyd."

"Alvina, you shore know how to make a feller feel welcome."

"Honey, you haven't seen nothing yet!"

For the next two nights Starbuck played the braggart. He took a room at the hotel in Liberty; but he saw it only during daylight hours. By dark each evening, he was johnny-on-the-spot at Ma Ferguson's bordello. And his nights were spent in Alvina's bed.

Starbuck drank heavily, and flung money around as if he owned a printing press. The effect, considering the mercenary nature of his hostess, was somewhat predictable. Ma Ferguson accorded him the deferential treatment reserved for big spenders, and saw to it that his glass was never empty. She also allowed him to monopolize Alvina. The charge, which included sleeping over, was a mere twenty dollars a night.

Outwardly bluff and hearty, Starbuck acted the part with a certain panache. Sober, he appeared to be a happy-go-lucky drifter, with some mysterious, and inexhaustible, source of funds. With several drinks under his belt, he then turned garrulous, pretending the loose tongue of an amiable drunk. Whores were accustomed to braggarts who seemed possessed of some irresistible urge to toot their horn and confide their innermost secrets. So Alvina found nothing unusual in Floyd Hunnewell's boastful manner, and she dutifully portrayed the spellbound listener. He told her a tale of outlandish proportions.

Improvising as he went along, Starbuck intertwined fact with fabrication. His story, unfolding in bits and pieces, was recounted with an air of drunken self-importance. A Texan born and bred, he'd worked as a cowhand since boyhood. Over the years, he had trailed herds to every cowtown on the Kansas plains. Then, after last summer's drive to Dodge City, he awoke to the fact that he was getting no younger, and no richer. Determined to make something of himself, he looked over the field and decided that horse stealing was an enterprise with real potential. For the past seven months, he had averaged better than fifty head a month, and it was all profit. In total, he had cleared more than ten thousand and no end in sight. A minor error in judgment had put the law on his tail, but that was no great calamity. He could afford to lie low and let the dust settle. Meanwhile, he was scouting around for a new venture, something befitting a man of his talents. Horse stealing, he'd decided, was too easy. A fellow who wanted to get ahead had to raise his sights—aim higher!

Alvina bought the story. It was, after all, no great shocker. Cowhands turned outlaw were fairly commonplace, and a horse thief in her bed was no cause for excitement. She'd slept with worse—lots worse—and never given it a thought. Yet she hadn't slept with anyone lately who was as much fun as Floyd Hunnewell. For all his crowing and cocksure conceit, he was damned likable. And to her surprise, he was a regular ball of fire in bed. The last couple of nights, she'd actually found herself enjoying it. Which was something to ponder.

To Starbuck, it was all in a day's work. Alvina was good company—gullible like most whores—and he was pleased that she'd swallowed his fairytale so readily. But that wasn't the reason he had selected her over the other girls, and stuck with her for two nights running. Instead, he'd zeroed in on her because she was by far the prettiest girl in Ma Ferguson's henhouse. Some gut instinct told him that her pert good looks would make her the favorite of one or more of the Younger brothers. By and by, he meant to turn that to advantage.

Late the third evening, Starbuck was seated on one of the sofas with Alvina. They were talking quietly, sipping whiskey, but his mind was elsewhere. The thought occurred that he might be in for a long wait. So far there had been no sign of the Youngers, and he'd heard no mention of their name. For all he knew, they might have taken their trade to another whorehouse. Or even worse, they could be off robbing a bank—and ready to hightail it for the Nations. By his count, they were already some months overdue at Belle Starr's. Still, there was nothing for it but to curb his impatience and wait it out. Time would tell, and meanwhile Alvina was a pleasant enough diversion. A damn sight more pleasant than that ax-faced bitch he'd wooed at Younger's Bend.

Alvina suddenly stiffened. She caught her breath in a sharp gasp and stared past him toward the door. He turned and saw three men enter the parlor. Though no photographs or drawings existed, the men fitted the general description of the Younger brothers. One of them separated, walking in the direction of the sofa while the other two continued on to the bar. He was powerfully built, with a pockmarked face, coarse sandy hair, and the bulge of a pistol beneath his coat. He halted, nodding to Alvina.

"How's things?"

"Fine." Alvina appeared flustered. "You haven't been around much lately."

"Well, I'm here now. C'mon, we'll have a drink and get ourselves caught up."

"Cousin," Starbuck interrupted politely. "You've done stopped at the wrong pew. The lady's taken for the night."

"Who says?"

"I reckon I do." Starbuck uncoiled slowly and got to his feet. " 'Specially since I paid for the privilege."

"The night's young. You just get in line, and when I'm done, she's all yours."

Starbuck sensed opportunity, and seized it. "Cousin, you must've heard wrong—"

"I've heard all I wanna hear! Close your trap or I'll close it for you."

"Say, looky here." A cocked sixgun emerged like a magician's dove from inside Starbuck's jacket. He scowled, and wagged the tip of the barrel. "I don't much cotton to threats. Suppose you just haul it out of here before I get tempted to make your asshole wink."

"Omigawd!" Alvina jumped to her feet. "Floyd, put it away! Please, honey, I'm asking—"

"Why the hell should I?"

"Because," Alvina whispered, touching his arm. "That's Jim Younger! The big one at the bar is Cole Younger, and the other one is Clell Miller. They'll kill you if you don't back off!"

"Younger?" Starbuck gave her a look of walleyed amazement. "Are you talkin' about *the* Younger brothers?"

"In the flesh," Alvina acknowledged. "Now cool down and play it smart! Like he told you, the night's young."

Starbuck shook his head in mock wonder. Then he

lowered the hammer and slowly holstered the Colt. With a lame smile, he glanced at Jim Younger.

"Any friend of Alvina's is a friend of mine."

Younger grunted, and roughly pushed Alvina toward the door. Without a word, she led the way into the hall and they mounted the stairs to the second floor. Starbuck watched after them a moment, trying his damnedest to look unnerved and properly chastised. After a time his gaze shifted to the bar, and he found himself pinned by Cole Younger's stare. He grinned weakly and walked forward, halting a pace away.

"No offense." He stuck out his hand. "Name's Floyd Hunnewell, and I shore don't want no trouble with the Youngers."

Cole ignored the handshake. "You're pretty sudden with a gun."

"Wisht I wasn't sometimes."

Cole regarded him evenly. "You keep pullin' guns on people and somebody's liable to give you a try."

"Hope there's no hard feelings." Starbuck looked painfully embarrassed. "I'd shore admire to buy you a drink, Mr. Younger."

"I guess not," Cole said bluntly. "We're sort of choosy about who we drink with."

"Well, maybe another time. I wouldn't want you to think I was unsociable, Mr. Younger."

"I'll keep it in mind."

Starbuck turned and walked back to the sofa. He was conscious of Ma Ferguson's beady glare and an almost palpable sense of tension among the girls. With a hangdog expression, he took out the makings and began rolling a smoke. He made a show of nervously spilling tobacco, and took two tries to light a match. Yet inside he was laughing, positively jubilant.

By sheer outhouse luck, he'd made an impression the Youngers would never forget. The suddenness of his draw—his willingness to resort to gunplay—all that would stick in their minds. Then, too, there was

Alvina. Even now, she was probably spilling his story to Jim Younger. And soon enough the word would circulate. Floyd Hunnewell was a wanted man, a horse thief with his eye on bigger things.

All in all, Starbuck thought he'd made a helluva start.

Chapter Ten

"We've got ourselves a real stem-winder this time!"

"Why's that?"

"Have a look and you'll see."

Bob Younger, recently returned from Minnesota, unfolded a hand-drawn map. The men were gathered around the dining table in the Hudspeth home. Jesse and Frank sat at opposite ends of the table, with Cole on one side and Bob, flanked by Jim, on the other. Bob spread the map in the middle of the table, and everyone leaned forward for a better look. A series of lines, radiating outward like spokes in a wheel, converged on a central spot. He pointed with his finger.

"Here's Northfield. This wavy line's the Cannon River. Whoever named it ought've called it the curly-cue. Crookedest sonovabitch you ever saw!"

Jesse glanced up. "What's so important about a river?"

"Oh, nothin' much." Bob smiled lazily. "It just

splits Northfield clean down the middle, that's all."

"You're saying the town's divided by the river?"

"See that mark?" Bob indicated two parallel lines. "That's the Northfield bridge. The river runs roughly north-south and the bridge crosses it east to west. Separates the town pretty near half and half."

"So how's the town laid out?"

"Well, it's mostly houses on the west side of the bridge. Then you cross the bridge headed east and you come out smack-dab on the town square. That's the main business center, with a few stores and some such off on these sidestreets. On beyond that, there's more houses."

"Sounds like a fair-sized town."

"You ain't whistlin' Dixie!" Bob's mouth curled. "I had a few drinks in one of the bars, and got cozy with some of the locals. They told me the town's pushin' five thousand and still growin' strong."

No one spoke for several moments. Cole Younger, already briefed by his brother, sat without expression, waiting. Frank shot him a sidewise glance, then quickly looked away. Jesse stared at the map a long while, his features unreadable. Then, almost to himself, he finally broke the silence.

"That's considerable bigger than anything we ever tackled before."

"Bigger haul, too!" Cole said stoutly. "Wait'll Bob tells you about the bank."

"What about it?"

Bob leaned back, thumbs hooked importantly in his suspenders. "Them locals I talked to was regular civic boosters. Told me the bank was just about the biggest in southern Minnesota. Hell, it's even got a highfalutin name—the First National Bank!"

"Forget the name." Jesse gave him a sour look. "How's it fixed for money?"

"Plumb loaded!" Bob let loose a hoot of laughter. "Them barflies said it's got a vault the size of a barn.

And they wasn't lyin' either! I meandered over and had a look for m'self."

"You checked out the bank?"

"Figgered I might as well. It was a Saturday, and the town was crawlin' with farmers and their families. I just joined the crowd and waltzed in there nice as you please."

"Tell him about the vault," Cole prompted. "What you saw."

"Well, now!" Bob snapped his suspenders and grinned. "The people was lined up three deep and depositin' money hand over fist. Seems like Saturday is the day all the farmers and folks from neighborin' towns does their business. You never saw nothin' like it in all your born days!"

"The vault," Jesse reminded him. "Did you get a look or not?"

"I did for certain! The door was standin' wide open, and you could've drove a wagon through the inside with room to spare. Ever' wall was lined with shelves and drawers, and the whole kit 'n' caboodle was stacked knee deep with money. Goddamnedest sight I ever laid eyes on!"

"How much would you estimate?" Jesse eyed him keenly. "Just a rough calculation?"

"Well, don't you see—" Bob spread his hands in an expansive gesture. "Folks come from all over to do their bankin' there 'cause it'd take a cannon to blow the door off that vault. The locals told me nobody'd ever tried a holdup. Not once!"

"Answer the question," Cole said with weary tolerance. "You done told me and Jim. Now tell Jesse. How much?"

Bob swallowed, licked his lips. "I'd judge two hundred thousand. As God's my witness, Jesse—not a penny less!"

Jesse shoved his chair away from the table. He rose and without a word walked to the parlor, where he began pacing back and forth in front of the fireplace.

Silence thickened at the table, and the men tracked him to and fro with their eyes. His head was bowed, thinking private thoughts, and a minute or longer passed before he suddenly stopped. Then he turned and moved once more to the table, standing behind his chair. His expression was somber, and determined.

"I don't like it." He punctuated the statement with a vigorous gesture. "There's got to be a reason that bank's never been robbed. Somebody would've tried —especially with all that money layin' around—unless there was a damn good reason. I say we scotch the idea right here and now."

"No!" Cole's jaw jutted stubbornly. "We've waited a lifetime for this kind of payday. Just because nobody else has busted that bank don't mean it can't be done. And that sure as hell ain't no reason for us not to try!"

Jesse was very quiet, eyes boring into him. "Cole, I've spoke my piece. I say it's a washout, and that's that."

Cole's bushy eyebrows seemed to hood his gaze. "Last time we met, I told you the Youngers wouldn't play tin soldier no more. That goes double after hearin' what Bob saw at Northfield."

"Suppose you spell that out a little plainer?"

"Since you asked—" Cole smiled with veiled mockery. "We're fed up with nickel-and-dime jobs, and we're through playin' it safe. If you haven't got the stomach for Northfield, then we'll just handle it our own selves."

A stony look settled on Jesse's face. "You sorry goddamn ingrate! I ought to kill you where you sit."

"Maybe you ought to," Cole challenged him, "but you won't. The way it stands now, you'd have to fight all us Youngers—not just one."

"Don't tempt me! Haulin' your ashes might make it worth it!"

Cole flipped his hand in scorn. "You love yourself

too much for that, Jesse. So I don't guess I'm gonna lose any sleep over it."

"By Christ—!"

"Not Christ," Frank interrupted, clearing his throat. "To quote the Bard: 'Hell is empty and all the devils are here.' You two make the line sound prophetic."

Jesse and Cole stared at him blankly. When neither of them responded, he went on. "Why in thunder do you have to fight? We've got enough enemies without turning on one another." He paused, then continued in a temperate voice. "Jess, I'm not taking sides; but you have to face the facts. Unless you bend a little, Cole and the boys will take off on their own. Once it comes to that, we'll likely never get it healed. So maybe you ought to make allowances. We've been together a long time."

Jesse was white around the mouth, his temples knotted. Yet he held his temper, avoiding Frank's steady look, and gave the matter some thought. "All right," he said finally, squaring himself up. "We'll lay out the job and get on with it. But once we're in Northfield—if it don't smell right or anything looks queer, I'll call it off and no questions asked. That's as far as I'm willin' to bend, no farther. So take it or leave it."

The Younger brothers swapped quick glances among themselves. At length, Cole nodded and swiveled his head just far enough to meet Jesse's venomous glare. "I guess we could go along with that. You always said Bob was the best scout in the bunch, and Northfield didn't give him the willies. Don't expect it will you either. Specially when you get a gander at the vault."

"If we get that far," Jesse said, watching him with undisguised hostility. "Just remember, once we're there, I call the tune as to whether or not we hit the bank. That's the deal."

"You want a blood oath?" Cole cracked a smile. "Or will my word do?"

Jesse let the remark pass. He seated himself, then

reached out and pulled the map closer. "Bob, show me the layout. Let's start with the bank."

"Sure thing, Jesse." Bob leaned forward, explaining various marks on the map. "The bank's over here at the east end of the square. Sits right on a corner, where the square leads into Division Street. I figgered the best approach was to come into town from the east—that means we'd be headed west on Division Street—and stop right in front of the bank. That way we can cover the square without exposing ourselves, and we've got nothin' behind us but a few stores. When the job's done, we just turn around and ride out the same way we came in. It's the shortest and safest route, near as I could tell."

"The shortest, maybe." Jesse studied the map with a critical eye. "Not necessarily the safest."

"I don't follow you."

"Your way we've only got one line of retreat. If we were discovered—and these shopkeepers back here on Division Street got up in arms—then we'd be caught between them and the ones on the square. In other words, they'd have us trapped in a bottleneck. I can't say I'd care too much for that idea."

"By gum, you got a point there."

"Where's the town marshal's office?"

"Over here." Bob pointed with a dirty fingernail. "Off the south side of the square, just round the corner."

"Which means he steps out his door and he's roughly kitty-corner to the bank."

"Yeah, I reckon it does."

"What's along the other sides of the square?"

"Oh, just the general run of businesses and shops. Couple of cafés and that saloon I mentioned. A hotel over on the north side, right about in the middle of the block. Course, down here, on the west side, there's not much of anything. Don't you see, that leads directly to the bridge."

"How wide is the bridge?"

"Well, it'll take two wagons abreast. Looked like they built it specially for the farm trade."

"Across the river"—Jesse directed his attention to the western shoreline—"you show a road headed south. What's down that way?"

"Nothin' much. The road generally follows the river, and a couple of miles south there's a crossroads called Dundas. After that, you hit a long stretch of woods. Then maybe ten miles south there's a fair-sized town called Faribault."

"What's west of those woods?"

"I brought back maps of Minnesota and Iowa. You want me to show you in detail?"

"Later," Jesse said shortly. "For now, just tell me about those woods."

"To the west, there's more of the same. Broken woods, with marshy terrain and lots of small lakes. Due west—maybe thirty miles—there's a town called St. Peter and southwest there's one called Mankato."

Jesse abruptly switched back to the Northfield bridge. "From here, are there any telegraph lines runnin' south?"

"No, there ain't." Bob pondered a moment. "I guess the towns are too small down that way. Near as I recollect, the poles all took a northerly direction—to Minneapolis."

"Thought so," Jesse said, almost to himself. "Now tell me about the bank. How's it laid out inside?"

Bob took a stub pencil from his coat pocket. Turning the map over, he began sketching a diagram on the opposite side. Watching them, Cole marveled at Jesse's tactical genius. Always the guerrilla commander, he saw any job along the lines of a military raid. Before an actual date was set for the job, he would have worked out every detail, including their route to Minnesota and the order of retreat once they'd robbed the bank. However grudgingly, Cole had to admit there were none the equal of Jesse James when it came to planning a holdup. The end result would be a textbook study in how to rob a bank and make a clean getaway. All without losing a man or exposing themselves to unnecessary risk.

After studying the floor plan of the bank, Jesse flipped over to the map. He briefly scanned the drawing of Northfield, then nodded to himself in affirmation.

"Here's the way I see it." His finger stabbed out at the map. "That bridge is the key point. Once we occupy it and hold it, we have a clear field of fire that covers the entire square. On top of that, our best line of retreat is south along the road to that stretch of woods. So everything hinges on taking control of the bridge."

"Lemme understand," Cole said, hunching forward for a look at the map. "You're sayin' somebody posted at the bridge could keep the townspeople pinned down while we're in the bank. Is that it?"

"Yeah, that's the first step. Course, we'll also need covering fire when we leave the bank and head back across the square. So like I said—that bridge has got to be held the whole time."

"No question there," Cole agreed. "What about the bank itself?"

"We'll split up into groups." Jesse tapped the map with his finger. "One at the bridge and another outside the bank. Between them, they'll have the square covered in a crossfire from one end to the other. Once they're in place, the third group will enter the bank and pull the job."

"Hold on!" Cole protested. "That'll split us up pretty thin, won't it?"

"Normally it would," Jesse said levelly. "Except I'm figurin' on eight men altogether. Three at the bridge, two outside the bank, and three more inside. With the size of the town, and the way it's laid out, I wouldn't try it with any less."

"So you're talkin' about three more besides ourselves?"

"That's the general idea."

"Well, I don't like it! That means we're gonna have to divvy out eight shares instead of five."

"Either we do it right or we don't do it at all. It'll take eight men to make certain we hold that bridge. And without the bridge—I'm not settin' foot in Northfield!"

"Whereabouts you figure to get 'em? There ain't a helluva lot of men I'd trust to cover my backsides."

"What about Clell Miller?" Bob suggested. "He pulled his weight on that last train job."

"Don't forget Charlie Pitts," Jim added quickly. "He's no slouch either."

"I suppose they'll do," Cole grumbled. "Now try thinkin' of another one that's worth his salt! All the good ones are dead or else they've turned tame as tabby cats."

"Not all," Frank said with a slow grin. "The way Jim tells it, there's a fellow down at Ma Ferguson's who acts more like a bobcat."

"Awww, hell, Frank!" Jim groaned. "I told you that private. Besides, he sucked wind quick enough when push came to shove."

"Only because you had Cole and Clell Miller to back your play."

"Wait a minute," Jesse broke in. "Who're you talkin' about?"

"Some stranger." Jim shrugged it off. "Him and me got into it over a girl, and he pulled a gun. Wasn't all that much to it."

"Tell me anyway," Jesse persisted. "Who is he? What d'you know about him?"

"He's a smalltime horse thief. Alvina, that's the girl, told me the law run him out of Kansas. Way he acts, he's had lots of experience runnin'."

"Bullfeathers!" Frank laughed. "You told me he got the drop on you so fast you never knew what happened. Anybody that handy with a gun, maybe we ought to consider him for the third man."

"God a'mighty!" Cole blustered. "You got rocks in your head, Frank. The man's an outsider."

"Cole, answer me this," Jesse said in a cold, dry manner. "What were you doing at Ma Ferguson's in the first place? I thought we agreed you'd stay clear of there."

"No such thing!" Cole muttered. "I told you I'd stay out of trouble—and I did!"

"The hell you did! A man pullin' a gun sounds like the kind of trouble we could do without."

"Jesus Christ! He pulled on Jim, not me!"

Jesse eyed him in disgust. "Maybe Frank's right. We could use some new blood in this outfit. 'Specially a rooster that'd pull on the Youngers."

"Whoa back, Jess." Frank gave him a troubled look. "I was only joking around. Why take it out on Cole?"

"Why not?" Jesse said with heavy sarcasm. "Anybody Cole don't like probably deserves a second look. You go on down to Ma Ferguson's and check out this horse thief. He might be just the man we need."

"You're makin' a mistake," Cole said sullenly. "And you know goddamn well you're only doing it to spite me."

"C'mon now!" Jesse mocked him. "You mean to say you don't trust Frank's judgment?"

"That ain't what we're talkin' about here."

"What are we talkin' about, then?"

"The same old thing." Cole's jaw muscles worked. "Who beats the drum and who winds up playin' tin soldier."

"Cole, I do believe you got the message."

"You're liable to thump your drum one of these days and nobody'll answer muster."

A ferocious grin lit Jesse's face. "There's lots of tin soldiers, Cole. But I'm the only one that's got a drum . . . and I aim to keep it!"

Chapter Eleven

"You shouldn't be so impatient, lover."

"Hell, I need some action! Fun's fun, but a steady diet of it don't suit my style."

"Thanks a lot!" Alvina crinkled her nose in a pout. "You sure know how to make a girl feel special."

"Holy moly!" Starbuck rolled his eyes upward. "I done spent six nights in a row with you! If that don't make you special, I shore as the devil don't know what would."

"A little sweet talk wouldn't hurt. You were full of it up until tonight."

"Yeah, you're right." Starbuck's tone was grumpy, out of sorts. "It's just that a feller goes stale after a while. Not that you ain't good company! I got no complaints on that score, none a 'tall. But it's like I'm gettin' itchy—and don't know where to scratch."

"Ooo." Alvina clucked sympathetically, kissed him softly on the cheek. "Don't get down in the mouth, sweetie. I told you I'd talk to Jim, and I will. Cross my heart!"

"Probably won't do no good," Starbuck said glumly. "Them Youngers ain't the friendliest bunch I ever run acrost."

"You leave it to me," Alvina assured him brightly. "Jim Younger thinks more of me than he does his own wife! One way or another, I'll convince him to at least talk to you."

"Well, I shore as hell wisht he'd show again! I'm plumb tuckered out with sittin' on my duff."

Starbuck's gruff manner was no act. Seated beside Alvina on a sofa, he watched listlessly as the evening crowd began drifting into Ma Ferguson's. The ivory tickler was playing a melancholy tune on the piano, and it somehow suited his mood. For the past three nights—since the evening he'd braced Jim Younger —he had planted himself on the sofa and waited. Some inner conviction told him the Youngers would return, and he'd kept himself steeled to take the next step in his plan. Yet tonight his conviction was waning rapidly. Unless the outlaws put in an appearance soon, then it was all wishful thinking. Not a plan but rather a pipe dream. He dully wondered if he'd sold himself a bill of goods.

"Don't you worry, Floyd." Alvina lowered one eyelid in a bawdy wink. "Where Jim Younger's concerned, I'm the hottest stuff in Clay County! He couldn't stay away if his life depended on it."

"Looks like he's making a pretty good stab at it."

"Oh, pshaw! You know what my mama used to say?"

"What's that?"

"She used to say, 'Worry is the curse of those who borrow trouble.' "

"I ain't worried," Starbuck grumbled. "It's like I told you—I'm just tryin' to scratch that itch."

"Well, I can't see why you're so stuck on becoming a bank robber anyway. The notion probably wouldn't have occurred to you in a thousand years if you hadn't bumped into the Youngers the other night."

"Who knows? I was lookin' for a new line of work and they just happened along at the right time. Nothing ventured, nothing gained."

"From what Jim tells me, they've ventured a lot and gained a little here lately. Talk about a bunch that needs a rabbit's foot!"

"He tells you all his secrets, does he?"

Alvina giggled and batted her eyelashes. "Honey, you just wouldn't believe it! I told you he was sweet on me."

"So their luck's turned sour, then?"

"Let's say they're not exactly rolling in clover."

"Hell, maybe you're right," Starbuck said guilefully. "Maybe robbin' banks ain't what it's cracked up to be."

"Feast or famine, that's the way it looks to me."

"I guess I could always go back to Kansas. Things have likely cooled off by now, and horse stealing ain't all that bad. Least it's regular work."

"Floyd!" Alvina looked wounded. "You said you liked it here!"

"I do," Starbuck said earnestly. "That's why I asked you to put in the word with Younger. But now, you sound like you're tryin' to talk me out of it."

"No, I'm not!" Alvina snuggled closer on the sofa. "You just put Kansas out of your mind. And stop worrying about Jim Younger! I'm one girl that doesn't go back on a promise."

Starbuck felt only a twinge of conscience. He had purposely set out to win her over, and six nights in her bed had proved adequate to the job. He'd treated her with gentleness and affection, and seen to it that their lovemaking was a thing of ardor rather than passionless rutting. All of which was like catnip to a working whore. She'd fallen for him very much in the manner of a schoolgirl surrendering her virginity. And recruiting her to his cause had been accomplished with surpassing ease.

Having failed in his approach to Cole Younger,

he'd thought to hedge his bet with Alvina. Her assis-
ance created a couple of intriguing possiblities. For
openers, she was a veritable fund of information. As
she herself had noted, men often confided more in
whores than in their own wives. Apparently that was
the case with Jim Younger, and whatever tidbits she
gleaned would be a welcome addition to the file. Of
greater import, she claimed some influence over
Younger. In the event she persuaded him to vouch for
Floyd Hunnewell, then the larger part of the problem
would be resolved. One recommendation would lead
to another, forming a daisy chain that would ultimately lead to Jesse James. From there, it would remain but a matter of time—and opportunity.

Starbuck by no means felt sanguine. Alvina might
prove an asset, and then again her efforts might very
well come to nothing. Yet, from his standpoint, there
was everything to gain, with little or no risk of exposing his hand. She was an unwitting operative—
undercover in every sense of the word—and more val-
uable for it. Should she prove ineffective, then it
would have cost him nothing more than six nights of
ardent lovemaking. And in all truth, the expenditure
had required no labor. He'd thoroughly enjoyed himself.

"See!" Alvina suddenly hissed out of the corner of
her mouth. "I told you he couldn't stay away!"

She popped off the sofa and hurried toward the
door. As Starbuck watched, she greeted Jim Younger
with an exuberant laugh and a teasing peck on the
mouth. Behind him, crowding through the doorway,
were Cole and two other men. One of them, not unlike the third pea in a pod, was clearly Bob Younger.
The other newcomer was slimmer of build, somewhat
gangling, with a determined jaw and a neatly trimmed
beard. Something about him bothered Starbuck. A wisp
of recognition that was at once familiar and elusive.

The men walked to the bar, with Alvina hanging
on Jim Younger's arm. None of them so much as

glanced at Starbuck, and he pretended to mind his own business. After a couple of drinks, Jim ordered a bottle from the barkeep; with Alvina in tow, he excused himself and led her toward the hallway. Cole, his voice loud and boisterous, subjected them to a coarse ribbing as they crossed the parlor. Arm in arm, ignoring his jibes, they disappeared up the stairs. Cole laughed uproariously and turned back to his companions. He whacked the bar, ordering a fresh round of drinks.

Several minutes later, the bearded man abruptly shoved away from the bar. He walked directly to the sofa and halted. His eyes were friendly but sharp, very sharp. He nodded to Starbuck.

"Mind if I sit down?"

"Help yourself, cousin. It's a free country."

Starbuck had a feral instinct for the truth. His every sense alerted, and he warned himself to play it loose. For some reason as yet unrevealed, he was about to be put to the test. He knew he dare not fail.

"I'm told," the man said tentatively, "you go by the name of Floyd Hunnewell?"

"You're told right," Starbuck said with a raffiish smile. "Appears you've got the advantage on me."

"Most folks call me Frank."

"Well, I'll be jiggered!" Starbuck gave him a look of unalloyed amazement. "I ain't no mental wizard, but my ma didn't raise no dimdots neither. Something tells me you got a brother named Jesse."

Frank gazed at him for a long, speculative moment. "Let's talk about you. I understand you're from Kansas?"

"Now and then," Starbuck said, grinning. "The rest of the time I'm a Texican—and damn proud of it!"

"Strayed a mite far north, haven't you?"

Starbuck regarded him with an expression of amusement. "Women shore do talk, don't they?"

"How so?"

"Why don't we skip the guessin' game? Seems

pretty clear Alvina spilled the beans to Jim Younger, and now he's put the bee in your ear. So it boils down to you askin' questions when you already know the answers."

"You're right." Frank smiled genially. "Your ma didn't raise any dimdots."

"Only one thing troubles me." Starbuck leaned back, legs casually stretched out before him. "Why're you askin' me any questions atall?"

"You could be a Pinkerton." Frank let the idea percolate a few moments. "A stranger appears out of nowhere and passes himself off as a horse thief. If you were in my boots—wouldn't that tend to make you leery?"

"Pinkerton!" Starbuck said wonderingly. "I been called lots of things in my time, but never nothin' that low-down. Course, you wasn't exactly accusin' me"—he paused for effect—"or was you?"

Frank smiled in spite of himself. "Fast as you are with a gun, that'd be pushing my luck pretty far, wouldn't it?"

"Shore do regret that." Starbuck chuckled, stealing a glance at the bar. "Guess the Youngers was some put out, huh?"

"No harm done. Jim has a habit of crowding people when he shouldn't. Nobody faults you for pulling a gun . . . so long as you don't do it again."

"In that case—" Starbuck raised an uncertain eyebrow. "How come you and me are sittin' here playing ring-around-the-rosy?"

Frank cocked his head and studied Starbuck thoughtfully. "Jim was naturally curious, especially after you threw down on him so quick. He twisted Alvina's arm and she let it drop that you're on the run. Any truth to it?"

Starbuck wormed around on the sofa and flexed his shoulders. "I'll have to have m'self a talk with Alvina. Her arm twists a little too easy—regular goddamn blabbermouth!"

"She also said you're on the scout for a new line of work."

"So?"

"Wondered why," Frank said almost idly. "You seem to have done fairly well in the horse business."

"Simple enough," Starbuck said lighty. "I don't aim to scratch a poor man's ass all my life. There's ways to make lots more money—and lots faster, too!"

Frank gave him a swift, appraising glance. "Got anything particular in mind?"

"Why?" Starbuck asked, deadpan. "You offerin' me a job?"

"What if I was?"

"I'd still ask why. You don't know me from a hole in the ground, and I ain't exactly in your league. See what I mean?"

"Everybody has to start somewhere."

"That's a fact," Starbuck said slowly. "Howsomever, not everybody starts at the top. Sort of makes me wonder whether you're testin' the water—or what?"

The shadow of a question clouded Frank's eyes, then moved on. "Why don't you sit tight for a minute? I want to have a word with Cole."

Starbuck's expression revealed nothing. Yet he was astonished by the turn of events, searching for a reason where none seemed to exist. Frank rose, nodding to him, and walked to the bar. The conversation with Cole Younger was short, and heated.

"I sounded him out," Frank commenced guardedly, "and he strikes me as being on the level."

Cole nailed him with a sharp, sidelong look. "You're not serious—are you?"

"Why not?" Frank temporized. "He's smart and he's had experience dodging the law. And you saw for yourself, he's no tyro with a gun."

"Come off it!" Cole demanded churlishly. "The bastard's an outsider! I don't want no part of it."

"Then why are we here?"

" 'Cause I didn't want no trouble with Jesse! Besides, it gimme me a chance to get my wick dipped."

Frank's face grew overcast. "I think you're being shortsighted, Cole. We could use a good man on this job, and Hunnewell seems to fit the ticket."

"No sale!" Cole's headshake was emphatic. "I won't work with a stranger. You give him the nod and you can count me out! That goes for the boys, too."

Cole turned away, ending the discussion. He signaled Bob, and in short order they had each selected a girl. Without another word to Frank, they stalked from the parlor, trailed by a couple of blowzy whores, and mounted the stairs. Frank appeared slightly bemused, staring after them for several seconds. Then, with a hopeless shrug, he walked back to the sofa.

"Sorry, Hunnewell." He rocked his head from side to side. " 'The nature of bad news infects the teller.' "

"Come again?"

"A line from Shakespeare." Frank lifted his hands with a sallow smile. "I thought we could find a spot for you, but it seems I was mistaken. Maybe next time."

"Next time?" Starbuck repeated, genuinely confused. "What's that supposed to mean?"

"A figure of speech," Frank said evasively. "There's always a next time and a time after that. See you around."

On that cryptic note, Frank moved into the hallway and out the door. Starbuck simply sat there, stunned. He hadn't the least notion of what had transpired or why. Yet there was one thing about which he was utterly certain. He'd just been blackballed for membership in the James-Younger gang.

Late that night Alvina joined him in the parlor. The Younger brothers, drunk and raucous, had departed only a short while before. She looked some the worse for wear, somber and somehow distracted. With a heavy sigh, she dropped beside him on the sofa.

"Well, lover." She smiled wanly. "How's things with you?"

"Slow." Starbuck's smile was equally bleak. "Mighty slow."

"Sorry," Alvina apologized. "I couldn't get rid of him. Usually he doesn't drink all that much; but there wasn't anything usual about tonight. He damn near killed that whole bottle."

"Forget it," Starbuck said darkly. "You got a job to do, and nobody's blamin' you for that."

Alvina studied his downcast face. "Aren't you going to ask me what happened?"

"Happened with what?"

"With Jim Younger," Alvina reminded him. "I was supposed to talk to him . . . remember?"

"Oh, yeah." Starbuck seemed to lose interest. "How'd it go?"

"It didn't! The bastard got drunk as a skunk and I never had a chance to sound him out."

"Don't matter," Starbuck said miserably. "Too late anyway."

"Too late?" Alvina parroted. "Too late for what?"

"Too late for me!" Starbuck's tone suddenly turned indignant. "Frank James halfway gave me an invite to join up with 'em. Then Cole Younger put the quietus on it so fast it'd make your head swim. I was in and out before I knew what hit me!"

"Jeezus!" Alvina murmured. "You've had yourself some night, honeybun!"

"I suppose you could say that."

"Well, at least I know why Cole nixed you."

"You do?"

Alvina gave him a bright nod. "They're planning a job. That's why I couldn't get a word in edgewise with Jim. He got drunk and bragged himself blue in the face." She hesitated, put a hand on his arm. "Don't blame yourself, lover. As big as this job sounds, Cole wouldn't risk breaking in a new man."

"Just my luck." Starbuck suppressed a sudden jolt of excitement. "How big . . . or didn't he say?"

"Oh, he said all right! To hear him tell it, they'll all retire when this one's over."

"Sounds like an express-car job."

"No, it's a bank. A real *big* bank."

"Wouldn't you know it!" Starbuck cursed, slumped back on the sofa. "Whereabouts? Not that it matters a wholehelluva lot."

An indirection came into Alvina's eyes. "North-something-or-other. I think he said Northfield. Or maybe Northville. Tell you the truth, I wasn't listening too close. What a girl don't know can't hurt her."

Starbuck chanced one last question. "Northfield? Hell, that don't sound so big to me. Where's it at?"

"Search me, lover. He didn't say and I didn't ask! All night he just kept saying it was going to surprise the living bejesus out of the Pinkertons."

"Wonder what he meant by that?"

"Who knows?" Alvina murmured wearily. "You'll pardon my French . . . but I really don't give a fuck anyhow."

Starbuck knew then he would learn no more. Yet, with luck, he thought perhaps he'd learned enough. The germ of an idea took shape in his mind, and his pulse quickened. A bank, more so than most places, would make a fitting stage. And a final curtain for Jesse James.

He wondered if there was a morning train to St. Louis.

Chapter Twelve

Starbuck revised his plan. After sleeping on it overnight, he decided the delay of another day was of no great consequence. Speed, in the overall scheme of things, was less essential than maintaining his cover story.

He had no clear idea when the robbery would occur. Yet it seemed unlikely the gang would ride out within the next couple of days. The Youngers, after their binge of last night, would need time to recuperate. Then, too, Frank James had evidenced no sense of urgency in either his attitude or his curious offer. All that indicated the holdup would not take place for at least three days, perhaps more. And since Starbuck's own plan was based largely on guesswork, he felt the need to copper his bet.

For Floyd Hunnewell to disappear mysteriously would almost certainly arouse suspicion. All the more so in the light of Alvina's thoughtless revelations the night before. A bit of insurance seemed in order, and for the simplest of reasons. There was an outside possibility that Floyd Hunnewell would, by necessity, return to Ma Ferguson's. To do so—without getting killed in the process—would require that his credentials as a horse thief withstand scrutiny. On balance, then, it seemed wise to enlarge the original cover story with still another tapestry of lies.

To that end, Starbuck improvised a tale designed to touch a whore's heart. He appeared disgruntled, thoroughly crestfallen that he'd muffed his chance to join the James-Younger gang. A change of scenery, he explained, along with a little action, was needed to restore his spirits. He'd decided to return to his old haunts—a horse-stealing foray into Kansas which would last a week, perhaps longer, depending on circumstances. Then, with his funds replenished, he would hightail it straightaway back to Ma Ferguson's. It wasn't goodbye, he told Alvina, but merely a pause in the festivities. Upon his return, the party would resume right where they'd left off.

Alvina accepted the story at face value. She was sad, even a bit misty-eyed, but not without hope. When he departed around midmorning, she was convinced their separation would be of short duration. She peppered him with kisses, hugging him fiercely, and let go only when he stepped through the front door. Waving, bravely snuffling back her tears, she watched as he rode away. For a whore, whose memories were generally bereft of sentiment, it was a moment to be treasured. She was overcome by the odd sensation of a woman sending her man off to battle.

Starbuck turned his attention to the task ahead. Kansas City was less than twenty miles from Ma Ferguson's, and he arrived there early that afternoon. He left the gelding at a livery stable, paying a week's charges in advance, and emerged onto the street. For the next hour he circled through the downtown area, frequently doubling back, always looking over his shoulder. At last, satisfied he hadn't been followed, he went to the train station and collected a suitcase he'd checked the week before. A short while later he stepped into one of the town's busier hotels. There, registering under a false name, he took a room.

Upstairs, Starbuck paused only long enough to deposit the suitcase in his room. Then he quickly took possession of the bathroom at the end of the hall. With all the modern conveniences, including hot and cold running water, he set to work. Standing before the lavatory mirror, he peeled off the fake mustache and carefully scrubbed spirit gum from his upper lip. After undressing, he drew a scalding bath and lowered himself into the tub. The water slowly turned dark brown as he alternately lathered and rinsed his hair. A final washing, with his head directly under the tap, removed the last of the dye. When he inspected himself in the mirror, the transformation was complete. Floyd Hunnewell had been laid to rest.

Late that afternoon, Starbuck emerged from the hotel by a side exit. He caught a hansom cab and went straight to the train station. After dropping his bag at the checkroom, he purchased a ticket; then he swiftly mingled with the crowd. Only by a fluke would he have been recognized by anyone from Clay County; he was attired in his Denver clothes, and his hair was once again light chestnut in color. Still, there was always that off chance, and he'd learned long ago that too much caution was far healthier than too little. By train time, he felt reasonably confident he was in the clear. On the stroke of six he boarded the evening eastbound for St. Louis.

At the first stop, an hour or so down the line, Starbuck hopped off the train. He collared the station agent, handing him a scribbled message and a ten-dollar bill. The agent, impressed by his generosity, promised to send the wire the moment the train was under way.

The message was addressed to Otis Tilford.

Not long after sunrise the train pulled into St. Louis. Starbuck left the depot on foot and headed uptown. A walk in the brisk morning air took the kinks out of his muscles and revived him from a long night in the chair car. By the time he reached the corner of Olive and Fourth, he'd worked up an appetite.

A café catering to the early-morning breakfast trade caught his attention. He first used the washroom to splash sleep out of his eyes and scrub his teeth with soap and a thorny forefinger. Then he sat down to a plate of ham and eggs, with a side order of flapjacks. He topped off the meal with a cigarette and a steaming mug of black coffee. On the street again, he went looking for a barbershop.

By half past eight, he'd had a trim and a shave. He reeked of talcum powder and bay rum, and he felt positively chipper as he walked along Fourth toward Delmar. At the corner, he entered the Merchants & Farmers Bank Building. The elevator deposited him on the third floor, and a moment later he pushed through the door of the International Bankers Association. The receptionist, still masquerading as a drill sergeant, evidenced no surprise at his arrival. His wire had been slipped under the door early that morning and he was expected. She escorted him directly into Otis Tilford's office.

The banker was seated behind hs desk. He smiled and beckoned Starbuck forward. His eyes were strangely alert and his handshake was cordial. He motioned to a chair.

"I must say I'm delighted to see you, Mr. Starbuck. There for a while I began to wonder if you had fallen victim to foul play."

"Nothing like that," Starbuck said, seating himself. "I've been on the go since I left here, and not a whole lot to report. Up till now anyway."

"You have news, then?" Tilford leaned forward eagerly. "A break in the case?"

"Maybe," Starbuck allowed. "Maybe not. All depends on the next turn of the cards."

"I don't believe I follow you."

"Suppose I fill you in on what's happened?"

"Yes, by all means! Please do, Mr. Starbuck."

Starbuck began with the tenuous leads he'd unearthed from the Pinkerton file. From there, he briefly recounted his trip to Indian Territory and the night with Belle Starr. Then, touching only on salient details, he related how he had infiltrated Ma Ferguson's bordello. Apart from the cover story, he made no mention of the disguise or the alias he'd assumed. As a matter of security, he never revealed professional secrets to anyone, not even a client. He went on to tell of Alvina and the Youngers, and his gradual acceptance as a regular at the brothel. Then, finally, he spoke of his strange conversation with Frank James.

"I got close," he concluded. "But close don't count except in horseshoes. One word from Cole Younger put a damper on the whole works."

"Good Lord!" Tilford said, visibly impressed. "You were actually face to face with Frank James!"

"Closer than I am to you right now. With a little luck, I could've killed him and the Youngers there and then. Course, I never tried for the obvious reason. I figured you wanted Jesse or nobody."

"Quite correct," Tilford said briskly. "Nevertheless, you are to be commended, Mr. Starbuck. To my knowledge, no one—certainly no Pinkerton—has ever made personal contact with Frank James. Not to mention the Younger brothers—and all of them in the same room!"

"All of them except the one we're after."

"A masterful piece of work, nonetheless! How on earth were you able to gain their confidence?"

"The girl," Starbuck told him. "She was the key. Once I got her on my side, the rest just fell into place."

"I marvel that the Pinkertons never considered such an approach."

Starbuck gave him a cynical smile. "I'd guess the Pinks wouldn't talk the same language as whores."

"Perhaps not." Tilford appeared nonplused, and quickly dropped the topic. "Well, now, Mr. Starbuck! Where do we proceed from here?"

"I need some information, and I need it today."

"Exactly what sort of information?"

"Alvina—she's the girl I mentioned—let slip that the gang has a holdup planned. She wasn't certain, but she thought the name of the town was either Northfield or Northville. We've got to determine which it is—and where."

"Where?"

"What state."

"Are you telling me she gave no indication as to the state?"

"She couldn't," Starbuck replied. "She didn't know."

"And she wasn't precise as to whether it's Northfield or Northville?"

"She leaned toward Northfield. All the same, she wouldn't have sworn to it."

"So, then, we're faced with a conundrum of sorts, aren't we?"

"If that means a head-scratcher, then I'll grant you it's a lulu."

Tilford steepled his fingers, thoughtful. "A possible solution occurs to me. The American Bankers Association publishes a booklet listing all member banks. In addition, when we were organizing the International Association, we compiled a list of virtually every bank in the Midwest. Between the two lists, we might very well find the answer."

"Sounds good," Starbuck observed. "How long will it take?"

"I have no idea." Tilford rose fom his chair. "However, I will attend to the search personally. I daresay that will speed things along."

"Need some help?"

"Thank you, no." Tilford moved around his desk. "I'll put every available clerk on it immediately. Please make yourself comfortable, Mr. Starbuck."

With that, Tilford hurried out of the office. Starbuck took out the makings and began building himself a smoke. He creased a rolling paper, holding it deftly between thumb and forefinger, and sprinkled tobacco into it. Then he licked, sealing the length of the paper, and twisted the ends. He struck a match on his boot sole and lit the cigarette. Exhaling smoke, he snuffed the match and tossed it into an ashtray. He settled down to wait.

Several times over the next hour Tilford's receptionist popped in to check on him. She offered coffee, which he accepted, and refilled his cup on each trip. At last, with his kidneys afloat, he declined the fourth refill. A cup of coffee was nothing without a smoke, and he put a dent in his tobacco sack during the prolonged wait. He was lighting yet another cigarette as Tilford bustled through the door. In his hand, the banker held a single sheet of foolscap.

"I fear we've somewhat compounded the problem, Mr. Starbuck."

"Oh, how so?"

"See for yourself." Tilford seated himself, and placed the paper on the desk between them. "I regret to say the prefix 'North' is not all that uncommon."

Starbuck pulled his chair closer and scanned the paper. On it, printed in neat capital letters, was a list of five towns: NORTHFIELD, ILLINOIS. NORTHFIELD, MINNESOTA. NORTHVILLE, MICHIGAN. NORTHRIDGE, OHIO. NORTHWOOD, IOWA. His eye was drawn to the top of the list, and he briefly considered the two Northfields. Then he took a long, thoughtful draw on his cigarette.

"Illinois and Minnesota." The words came out in little spurts of smoke. "Guess we could toss a coin and hope for the best."

"Let me pose a question." Tilford studied his nails a moment. "Is it possible the girl was confused, somehow got the name of the town wrong?"

"Anything's possible," Starbuck remarked. "What makes you ask?"

"You will note"—Tilford tapped the paper—"there are five states listed there. Of those states, the James-Younger gang has been active in only one, that state being Iowa."

"You're saying there's a connection?"

"Precisely!" Tilford intoned. "For all his robberies, Jesse James had limited himself to a very defined territory. If nothing else, the Pinkertons established that every robbery occurred either in Missouri or in a state contiguous to Missouri."

"I'm not much on four-bit words."

"Contiguous," Tilford elaborated, "simply means a bordering state. In short, the James-Younger gang had *never* been known to operate in a state which did not directly border Missouri."

Starbuck again scanned the list. "You're telling me we ought to forget Minnesota, Michigan, and Ohio?"

"I am indeed," Tilford affirmed. "I seriously question that Jesse James would cross Iowa to rob a bank in Minnesota. Nor would he cross Illinois and Indiana to rob a bank in Michigan. It flies in the face of a record established over a period of seventeen years."

Starbuck was silent for a time. "I take it you've got a theory all worked out?"

"Facts speak for themselves," Tilford said with exaggerated gravity. "I submit the robbery will take place in one of two towns. The logical choice—based on what the girl was told—is Northfield, Illinois. A distant second, at least in my opinion, would be Northwood, Iowa."

"Northwood's out," Starbuck said in a low voice. "She wasn't certain, but she only mentioned two names: Northfield and Northville." He paused, slowly stubbed out his cigarette in the ashtray. "Tell me about Northfield, Illinois. What size town is it?"

"Quite small. I believe the population is something less than five hundred."

"Which means the bank wouldn't be any great shakes. How about Northfield, Minnesota?"

"Considerably larger," Tilford admitted. "I would judge it at roughly five thousand."

"And the bank?"

"Old and very prosperous," Tilford said, frowning heavily. "One of the largest in the Midwest."

There was a moment of weighing and deliberation before Starbuck spoke. "Alvina told me it was a big job, bigger than anything the gang had ever pulled. So that pretty well eliminates the bank in Illinois. To my way of thinking, it narrows down to one candidate— Northfield, Minnesota."

"I strongly disagree," Tilford said sharply. "Why would Jesse James travel that far to rob a bank? There's no logic to it! Absolutely none!"

"Outlaws aren't noted for logic. Even if they were, I'd have to follow my hunch on this one. Jesse and his boys are out to make a killing, and it was Jim Younger himself who said so. That speaks lots louder to me than all your facts."

"Are you prepared to stake your reputation on a hunch, Mr. Starbuck?"

"Why not?" Starbuck said with sardonic amusement. "Except for hunches, I would've been dead a long time ago."

"And in the event logic prevails . . . what then?"

"Tell you what." Starbuck met his look squarely. "You alert the authorities at Northfield, Illinois. Meantime, I'll get myself on up to Minnesota. That way everybody's happy."

"Compromise was hardly what I had in mind."

"It's all you'll get," Starbuck said quietly. "I told you when I signed on . . . I do it my way or I don't do it at all."

There was an awkward pause. Tilford's features congested, and his mouth clamped in a bloodless line. "Very well," he conceded at length. "When will you leave?"

"First train out," Starbuck informed him. "I like to scout the terrain before I lay an ambush."

"Ambush!" Tilford looked upset. "Won't the authorities in Minnesota have something to say about that?"

"All depends."

"On what, may I ask?"

"On whether or not I tell them."

"Good God!" Tilford shook his head in stern disapproval. "Surely you don't intend to take on the entire gang—without assistance!"

"We'll see." Starbuck gave him a devil-may-care grin. "Sometimes it's easier to kill a man by operating alone. Northfield might be too civilized for *our* kind of justice."

Tilford could scarcely mistake the nature of the grin, or the words. He had, after all, hired a man to dispense summary justice. Northfield's wishes in the matter were wholly immaterial.

"Yes." His tone was severe. "You may very well have a point, Mr. Starbuck."

Starbuck unfolded slowly from his chair. He tugged his jacket smooth and walked to the door. Then, as he was about to step into the hall, he paused and looked back over his shoulder. A ghost of a smile touched his mouth.

"I'll let you know how it comes out."

Chapter Thirteen

Starbuck stood on the veranda of the Dampier House Hotel. A cigar was wedged in the corner of his mouth and his hands were locked behind his back. Under a noonday sun, he puffed thick clouds of smoke and stared out across the square. His gaze was fixed on the First National Bank.

Only an hour before, upon arriving in town, Starbuck had checked into the hotel. He was posing as a sundries drummer, whose territory had recently been broadened to include Minnesota. Apart from the ubiquitous cigar, his attire was the uniform of virtually all traveling salesmen. He wore a derby hat and a snappy checkered suit with vest to match. A gold watch chain was draped across the vest, and a flashy diamond ring sparkled on his pinky. His physical appearance was unchanged, with the exception of an old standby.

A gold sleeve, crafted with uncanny workmanship, was fitted over his left front tooth. The overall effect, as with any subtle disguise, was principally one of misdirection. When he smiled, which was a drummer's stock in trade, people seldom saw his face. Their recollection was of a gold tooth and a steamy cigar. The man who called himself Homer Croydon was otherwise lost to memory.

Today, eyes squinted in concentration, Starbuck was performing a feat of mental gymnastics. A manhunter who survived soon acquired the knack of looking at things from an outlaw's perspective. Long ago, the trick had become second nature, and he was now able to step into the other fellow's boots almost at will. Visualizing himself to be Jesse James, he pondered on a foolproof way to rob the bank.

Based on all he'd learned, Starbuck knew it would be a mistake to think in conventional terms. Jesse James, unlike most bank robbers, approached each job as though it were a military operation. The Pinkerton file rather conclusively demonstrated that the James-Younger gang was organized along the lines of a guerrilla band. Without exception, their holdups had been executed with a certain flair for hit-and-run. Surprise, as in any guerrilla raid, was the key element. Every step was orchestrated—planned with an eye to detail—and the gang generally made good their escape before anyone realized a robbery had occurred. That, too, indicated the meticulous preparation characteristic of each job. The retreat, and subsequent escape, was engineered with no less forethought than the holdup itself. And therein lay the mark of Jesse James' overall genius. In seventeen years, he had never been outfoxed. His trademark was a cold trail . . . leading nowhere.

Yet Northfield presented a unique tactical problem. Brooding on it, Starbuck slowly became aware that the situation was fraught with imponderables. The layout of the town did not lend itself to a hit-and-run raid. The square was open and broad, affording little in the way of concealment. On all sides, stores fronted the square; tradesmen and shopkeepers had a perfect view of the bank; any unusual activity would immedi-

ately draw their attention. The chances of discovery—
before the job was completed—were therefore in-
creased manyfold. In that event the odds also multi-
plied that the gang would be forced to fight its way out
of Northfield. Because the river bisected the town,
however, there were only two logical lines of retreat.
One led eastward, along Division Street, which began
on the corner where the bank was located. Yet, while
Divison Street was the quickest route of escape, any
flight eastward would merely extend the line of retreat.
Headed in the wrong direction, the gang would at
some point be compelled to double back on a south-
westerly course. For in the end, there was no question
they would make a run for Indian Territory.

The other escape hole was westward, across the
bridge. There, too, the tactical problem was apparent.
To reach the bridge, the gang would have to traverse
the entire length of the square. Should trouble arise,
and the townspeople take arms, the outlaws would be
forced to run a gauntlet of gunfire. At first glance, the
hazards entailed seemed to rule out the bridge. Still,
apart from surprise, the chief attribute of an experienced guerrilla leader was to do the unexpected when
it was least expected. A calculated risk at best, the
bridge might nonetheless offer the lesser of two evils.
It led westward, the ultimate direction of escape, and
it shortened the line of retreat by perhaps thirty or
forty miles. On balance, then, the advantages might
very well outweigh the hazards. No one would expect
a gang of bank robbers to take the hard way out of
town. Nor would they anticipate that the gang leader
might deliberately—

Starbuck was rocked by a sudden premonition. He
stepped off the veranda and crossed the block-long ex-
panse of the square. At the bridge, he halted and
stared for a moment at the houses on the opposite side
of the river. Then, on the verge of turning, his eyes
were drawn to the line of telegraph poles running
north. His gaze shifted south—no telegraph poles!—

and any vestige of doubt disappeared. Facing about, he subjected the square to cold scrutiny. From a tactical outlook, the bridge instantly became a key vantage point. The entire square, from end to end, was commanded by an unobstructed field of fire. There was, moreover, the element of the unexpected from where it was least expected. In the event fighting broke out, the townspeople would be looking toward the bank, not the bridge. And the outcome was easy to visualize.

Starbuck walked back to the hotel. Whether by deductive reasoning or swift-felt instinct, he knew he'd doped out the plan. Some inner certainty told him the holdup would proceed along the lines he'd envisoned. All that remained was to decide his own course of action. As he saw it, there were two options, both of which held merit. The critical factor was yet another of those imponderables.

To kill Jesse James all he had to do was bide his time. His room, which was on the second floor, fronted the hotel and directly overlooked the square. The range, from his window to the door of the bank, was roughly forty yards. No easy shot with a pistol, it was nonetheless one he had made many times before. By placing his gun hand on the windowsill—and holding high with the sights—he felt entirely confident of a kill shot. When the gang exited the bank, his shot was certain to go unnoticed in the ensuing gunfire.

Then, still posing as a drummer, he need only check out of the hotel and be on his way. Homer Croydon would be remembered by no one. Nor would anyone associate him with the death of Jesse James.

The alternative was to contact the town marshal. However, that route would require discretion and an oath of silence. Should the marshal prove the talkative sort—and word of an impending robbery spread through Northfield—then any hope of trapping the gang would be gravely jeopardized. The risk was compounded by the fact that others, by necessity, would be drawn into the scheme. Quite properly, the marshal would insist on alerting some of the townsmen. Extra guns, and men willing to use them, would be needed against a band of killers. Still, by stressing the need for secrecy, there was every reason to believe the plan would work. The welfare of Northfield and its citizens would be at stake. And trustworthy men, committed to the common good, could be persuaded to hold their silence.

In the end, Starbuck's decision had little to do with Northfield. He was concerned for the lives of innocent bystanders, and he had no wish to see the square turned into a battleground. Yet, for all that, his decision was a matter of personal integrity. While he had killed many men, he was no assassin. To hide, and shoot down a man from his hotel window, somehow went against the grain. His code in such matters was simple and pragmatic. He always gave the other man a chance, but he tried never to give him the first shot.

On reflection, it was the way he preferred to kill Jesse James. No stealth or potshots from hotel windows. He would do it openly, face to face—on the street.

Shortly after the noon hour, Starbuck left the hotel and crossed the square. Opposite the bank, he rounded the corner and walked toward the marshal's office, which was one door down. Northfield appeared to be a peaceful town, with nothing more serious than an occasional fistfight or a rowdy drunk. Other than the marshal, he thought it unlikely the town would employ any full-time officers. When he entered the office, his judgment was confirmed. All the cell doors stood open, and except for the marshal, the place was deserted. Seated behind a battered desk, the lawman was idly cleaning his fingernails with a penknife.

"Afternoon."

"Yessir." The marshal gave his gold tooth and snappy outfit a quick once-over. "Do something for you?"

"Are you Marshal Wallace Murphy?"

"I am." Murphy closed the penknife and stuck it in his pocket. "What's the problem?"

"No problem, Marshal. I was instructed to call on you when I got into town."

"Don't say?" Murphy looked flattered. "Who by?"

"Mr. Otis Tilford," Starbuck lied. "President of the International Bankers Association."

"Oh, yeah! Now that you mention it, the name rings a bell. Formed not too long ago, wasn't it?"

"Last summer," Starbuck said with a note of pride. "We're headquartered in St. Louis."

"I take it you work for the association?"

"In a manner of speaking. I'm a private detective, Marshal." Starbuck grinned and tipped his derby. "This drummer's getup is strictly window-dressing. I was hired as an undercover operative by Mr. Tilford."

"I don't believe I caught your name?"

"Luke Starbuck. Course, that's just between you and me. I'm registered at the hotel under the name of Homer Croydon."

Murphy was heavily built, with a square, thick-jowled face and a ruddy complexion. The chair squeaked under his weight as he leaned forward, elbows on the desk. He suddenly appeared attentive.

"Why all the secrecy?"

"Like I told you, I'm working undercover."

"So you did." Murphy eyed him with a puzzled frown. "What brings you to Northfield?"

"Well . . ." Starbuck let him hang a moment. "I need your word everything will be kept in the strictest confidence, Marshal. Otherwise I'm not at liberty to divulge the details of my assignment."

"I dunno." Murphy sounded uncertain. "If it's got to do with Northfield, that could put me in an awkward position."

Starbuck flashed his gold tooth. "I'd say it's more likely to make you the town hero. Hear me out and I think you'll agree I'm right."

Murphy nodded, digesting the thought. "Okay, fire

away. Only I warn you—I won't be a party to anything that's not in the best interests of Northfield."

"Fair enough." Starbuck's expression turned solemn. "Sometime within the next week, the First National Bank will be robbed."

"Robbed!" Murphy stared at him, dumbstruck. "How the hell would you know a thing like that?"

"How I know isn't important—"

"Says you!" Murphy cut him short. "You walk in off the street and tell me the bank's about to be robbed? I'll have an explanation, mister. And I'll have it damned quick."

"Suit yourself." Starbuck read a certain disbelief in his face, and decided to embellish the truth. "I was hired to infiltrate a gang of bank robbers. I located their hangout—a whorehouse—and I managed to get on chummy terms with them. Three nights ago, one of them got drunk and spilled the beans. So I checked with Mr. Tilford and he ordered me to contact you on the double. Here I am."

Murphy looked at him with narrow suspicion. "How do I know you're on the level?"

"If you don't believe me," Starbuck said lightly, "then just hide and watch. They're on their way to Northfield right now."

"Who's they?"

"Jesse James and the Youngers."

Murphy's mouth popped open. "Did you say Jesse James—*the* Jesse James?"

"The one and only."

"That's impossible!" Murphy shook his head wildly. "Why would Jesse James come all the way to Minnesota to rob a bank? It doesn't make sense!"

"Pay close attention, Marshal." Starbuck's eyes went cold and impersonal. "I don't have time to waste arguing with you. They're headed in your direction and that's a rock-solid fact. Now, I can show you how to stop them from robbing the bank, not to mention covering yourself with glory." He paused, jerked a thumb over his shoulder. "Or I can walk out that door and leave you with egg on your face. I reckon it all depends on how much you like wearing a marshal's badge."

"What the hell do you mean by that?"

"Why, it's pretty simple," Starbuck said without expression. "The town fathers wouldn't look too kindly on a man who let Jesse James ride in here and empty out the bank. All the more so once they heard Mr. Otis Tilford sent a special representative to warn you in advance."

There was a stark silence. Wallace Murphy stared down at his hands, tightlipped. He seemed to be struggling within himself, and several moments passed before he looked up. Then he dipped his head in affirmation.

"Go ahead, say your piece. I'm listening."

On impulse, Starbuck pressed the advantage. "One more thing. I call the shots from here on out. You can take all the credit, but I won't let you monkey with my plan. Understood?"

"Understood," Murphy agreed gingerly. "Only you better come up with something damn good."

"I already have," Starbuck said with an odd smile. "You see, Marshal—I know how they intend to pull the job."

"Big deal!" Murphy laughed uneasily. "What's to robbing a bank? You just walk in and pull a gun."

"Not Jesse James," Starbuck countered. "Him and his boys are old guerrilla fighters. So we're in for a military operation from start to finish."

"Would you care to spell that out?"

"For openers, a couple of the gang will post themselves somewhere near the bank door. They're the outside men, and their job is to keep the street clear. That way, there's less chance of trouble when it comes time for the getaway."

"In other words, they're the ones that'll show first?"

Starbuck nodded. "Once they're in position, then

Jesse and a couple more of the gang will enter the bank. We can depend on that. Jesse always handles the inside work himself."

"What's so unusual about that? Sounds fairly routine to me."

"There's an added touch," Starbuck said soberly. "At least two men, maybe more, will take control of the bridge. If trouble develops during the holdup, they'll keep everyone on the square pinned down with gunfire. Afterward, they'll cover the withdrawal when the bunch at the bank starts back across the square. Their last job is to act as a rear guard; fight a holding action at the bridge. Once the others are across the river and in the clear, then they'll take off like scalded ducks."

"Damn!" Murphy suddenly grasped it. "That means anybody who tangles with them would be caught in a crossfire. It'd be suicide to set foot on the square!"

"We'll let Jesse and his boys go right on thinking that. Meantime, we'll arrange a little surprise of our own."

"An ambush!" Murphy's eyes brightened. "By God, I like your style, Starbuck! How long you figure we've got?"

"Well, let's see." Starbuck pulled at his ear. "Tomorrow's Saturday, and they wouldn't risk it with the farm crowd in town. So I'd say the early part of the week, probably Monday."

"With seven or eight of them, we'll need some help with this ambush of yours."

"Not too many," Starbuck cautioned him. "The fewer involved, the less chance of word leaking out. Do you know three or four men who can be trusted to keep their mouths shut?"

"Oh, hell, yes!" Murphy chortled. "Half the men in Northfield would give their left nut for a crack at Jesse James."

"Hold it to three," Starbuck said firmly. "That's plenty for what I have in mind. And don't let the cat out of the bag! Arrange to get them together sometime tomorrow, and I'll explain the setup myself. I already know where I want them spotted."

"I guess that only leaves Fred Wilcox. He's the president of the bank. When do we give him the good news?"

"We don't."

"What?" Murphy went slackjawed with amazement. "Fred's got to be warned! You can't let that gang of murderers walk in there cold!"

"I don't aim to." Starbuck regarded him with a level gaze. "But we can't risk a bunch of nervous Nellies tipping our hand. We'll hit the minute Jesse steps down out of the saddle. So don't work yourself into a sweat. He'll never make it inside the bank—I guarantee it."

"Kill him dead!" Murphy cackled. "Shoot him down like a mad dog! That's what you're saying, isn't it?"

Starbuck smiled. "If a man's worth shooting, then I reckon he's worth killing."

"Like I said, Starbuck." Murphy chuckled heartily. "I admire your style."

"One last thing," Starbuck advised him. "I fire the first shot. That'll be the signal for you and your men to cut loose; but I don't want anybody to get over-eager. Agreed?"

"Agreed! You've got my word on it."

Wallace Murphy was tempted, but he let the question go unasked. He already knew the answer, and counted it no great surprise. Starbuck's presence in Northfield was explanation enough.

The first shot would be for Jesse James.

Chapter Fourteen

On Monday morning, the First National Bank opened at the usual time. Fred Wilcox, the president and chief stockholder, arrived a minute or so before eight. Waiting for him were the bank tellers, Joseph Heywood and Alan Bunker. He unlocked the front door and the men filed inside. A moment later the shade snapped up on the wide plate-glass window fronting the square.

Starbuck was seated on the veranda of the hotel. He pulled out his pocket watch and checked the time. The marshal had told him Wilcox was a punctual man, and he noted the window shade went up almost precisely on the stroke of eight. Around the square, following the banker's example, tradesmen began opening their doors. Northfield stirred and slowly came to life. To all appearances it was a typical Monday morning, unremarkable in any respect. The townspeople, suspecting nothing, went about the routine of another business day.

A cigar jutting from his mouth, Starbuck lazed back

in the cane-bottomed rocker. His legs were outstretched, heels planted atop the veranda railing, and
the derby was tipped low over his forehead. To passersby, he looked like a slothful drummer, sunning
himself after a heavy breakfast. In truth, he was alert
and observant, his eyes moving hawklike around the
square. He set the rocker in motion, ticking off a mental checklist item by item.

The three men selected by Marshal Wallace Murphy were already in position. Their weapons were se-
creted, but close at hand, and there was nothing about
them to draw undue attention. One, Arthur Manning,
operated a dry-goods store, located two doors north of
the bank. Another, Elias Stacey, was proprietor of the
town pharmacy. His shop was on the southeast corner
of the square, directly across Division Street from the
bank. The third man, Dr. Henry Wheeler, was stationed in Starbuck's second-floor hotel room. A crack
shot, widely known for his marksmanship, Doc Wheeler
was armed with a breech-loading target rifle. The marshal, whose office was kitty-corner from the bank, kept
a lookout from his window. His instructions were to
stay off the street and out of sight.

Early Saturday morning, the three men had been
summoned to the marshal's office. There, he had introduced them to Starbuck and briefed them on the
forthcoming holdup attempt. The men had listened
with dismay and shock, somewhat incredulous. Yet all
three were veterans of the Civil War, and no strangers
to bloodshed. Nor were they overawed that they were
being asked to take arms against the James-Younger
gang. They were, instead, filled with a sort of righteous
indignation. Jesse James was vilified as a murderous
blackguard, and each of them looked upon the defense
of their town and their neighbors as a civic duty. To
a man, they eagerly volunteered their services.

Starbuck had first sworn them to an oath of silence.
He impressed on them the need for absolute secrecy,
which included wives and friends and business ac-

quaintances. Jesse James, he noted, would be on guard for anything out of the ordinary; it was entirely likely a member of the gang would reconnoiter the town one last time before the robbery. With the point made, Starbuck then went on to the ambush itself. Their primary objective was the group of robbers—four or five in number—who would assemble outside the bank. These men were to be killed on the spot, before they had time to react and turn the square into a battleground. The men at the bridge, so long as they made no attempt to cross the square, were secondary. By concentrating on the bank, a dual goal would be served. The majority of the gang would be wiped out and the robbery would be aborted on the instant.

From there, Starbuck had proceeded to the matter of individual assignments. Manning and Stacey, whose stores were in direct proximity to the bank, were to arm themselves with shotguns. Caught between them, the robbers would be neatly sandwiched in a crossfire; their shotguns would sweep the sidewalk immediately outside the bank with a barrage of lead. The marshal, armed with a repeating rifle, would fire from the doorway of his office. His principal concern would be the outside team of robbers; once the firing became general, however, he would be free to select targets of opportunity. Doc Wheeler, whose target rifle was equipped with peep sights, would be responsible for the bridge. The gang members there were to be killed or pinned down, and thus neutralized. In that manner, they would be effectively eliminated from the larger fight.

Starbuck next outlined his own role in the ambush. Several of the gang members—notably Frank James and the three Younger brothers—were known to him on sight. The odds dictated that one or more of these men would be part of the outside team, the first contingent to approach the bank. Upon spotting them, he would leave the hotel veranda and cross to the south side of the square. His movement would alert Manning, Stacey, and Doc Wheeler that the holdup attempt was under way. Once across the square, he would then turn east and stroll toward the corner. By timing it properly, he would arrive at the corner as the second contingent rode up to the bank. One of these men was certain to be Jesse James, and along with the inside team he would dismount at the hitch rack. The moment they were on the sidewalk, and moving toward the door of the bank, Starbuck would open fire. His shot would be the signal for Marshal Murphy and the others to cut loose. With luck, the whole affair would be concluded in a matter of seconds.

Summing up, Starbuck had stressed the importance of a dispassionate attitude. He reminded the men that the James-Younger gang was a band of cold-blooded murders, prone to acts of savagery. He urged them to shoot to kill, and to continue firing until the last outlaw had been taken out of action. Any hesitation, any show of mercy, would only endanger innocent bystanders. To save the lives of friends and neighbors required that they kill quickly and efficiently. And with no regard to the aftermath.

Arthur Manning, perhaps having second thoughts, had then raised the issue of bystanders. In the event passersby happened along at the last moment or innocent parties got in the line of fire, he wondered if it might not be prudent to hold off, and let the gang rob the bank. At that point, he observed, when they were once again mounted and moving across the square, they could be ambushed in a relatively open area. Starbuck assured him that such a plan would result in random gunfire, and imperil the lives of everyone on the square. By containing the shooting to a limited zone—the front of the bank—there was less chance of someone catching a stray bullet. Doc Wheeler, whose usual business was saving lives, forcefully agreed. He advised Manning to leave tactics to Starbuck. The ambush, as laid out, was in his opinion their best hope. The others voiced assent, and the meeting had concluded on that note. Starbuck's plan would be followed to the letter.

To bolster their confidence, Starbuck had arranged a dry run later that afternoon. He waited until the farmers and their families began the trek homeward; with their departure, the Saturday crowds thinned out and the sidewalks became passable. Walking to the southwest corner of the square, he stopped and turned to face the bank. From there, he was in plain view of Doc Wheeler and the two tradesmen. He gave them the high sign, indicating he was satisfied with the arrangement. Then, cutting across the intersection on an oblique angle, he stepped off the distance to the bank entrance. By his stride, it was fourteen paces, roughly fifteen yards. He considered it an easy shot. One Jesse James would never hear.

Yet now, seated in the rocker, he wondered if today would be the day. Where Jesse James was concerned, there were few certainties, and a good deal of guesswork. Still, if a bank was to be robbed, then Monday was the ideal time. All morning, a steady stream of merchants and shopkeepers had trooped into the bank. Their receipts from Saturday's trade were heavy, and they were clearly anxious to get the money out of the stores and on deposit. Which made the bank a tempting target indeed. The vault would be stuffed with cash—and standing wide open.

As the noon hour approached, Starbuck experienced a moment of concern. If today was not the day, he knew he could expect problems with his squad of volunteers. Wallace was a peace officer, and therefore somewhat accustomed to the vagaries of manhunting. The others, despite their wartime service, were newcomers to the game. A professional soon learned that patience and determination were essential in any match of wits with outlaws. Amateurs, on the other hand, were quick to lose their taste for killing. The excitement—that initial surge of bloodlust—was short-lived. The longer the wait, the more time they had to think.

And given enough time, most men would talk themselves out of the notion. Unless the gang struck today, that might easily happen in Northfield. For the three townsmen, the act of cold and premeditated killing would begin to weigh heavily. Tomorrow or the next day—

All at once Starbuck alerted. His pulse quickened as he spotted Cole Younger and the man named Clell Miller ride over the bridge. Unhurried, holding their horses to a walk, they proceeded on a direct line across the square. Their eyes moved constantly, searching the stores and the faces of people on the street. Anything out of the ordinary—empty stores or too few people abroad—would immediately put them on guard. For the job to go off as planned, the town had to appear normal, nothing unusual or out of kilter. Otherwise they would simply turn and ride back across the bridge.

Starbuck sat perfectly still. From beneath the brim of his derby, he watched them ride past and plod on in the direction of the bank. He casually stood, stretching himself, and yawned a wide, jaw-cracking yawn. Then he bit off the tip of a fresh cigar and lit it with the air of a man savoring a good smoke. Stuffing the cigar in his mouth, he went down the hotel steps and meandered across the square. On the sidewalk, he turned and strolled aimlessly toward the corner. Ahead, he saw the two outlaws rein to a halt before the bank and dismount. Cole stooped down and pretended to tighten the saddle girth on his horse. Miller circled the hitch rack and stepped onto the sidewalk. With a look of bored indifference, he stood gazing out at the square.

Approaching the corner, Starbuck slowed his pace. Directly ahead, he spotted Stacey watching him through the window of the pharmacy. Out of the corner of his eye, he caught a glimpse of Manning leaning idly in the doorway of the dry-goods store. He stopped before a clothing emporium, playing for time, and made a show of peering at the window display. The hotel, now diagonally behind him, was mirrored in the reflection of the glass. He studied the window of his room, noting the lower pane was raised; through the gauzy curtains, the outline of Doc Wheeler was faintly visible. The men were in place and ready to act the instant he gave the signal. All that remained was for Jesse James to put in an appearance.

Starbuck puffed his cigar and bent closer to the window. He checked the bank in the reflection, troubled by what seemed an abnormal lapse of time. Cole and Clell Miller, still loafing outside the bank, were staring in the direction of the bridge. Starbuck turned his head slightly, and took a quick peek. His expression darkened, oddly bemused. Jim Younger, accompanied by two men unknown to him, cleared the east end of the bridge and reined their horses off to one side. They dismounted, reins gripped firmly, and stood as though waiting. Their eyes were fixed on the bank.

A sudden chill settled over Starbuck. Something about the setup was wrong, all turned around. The way he'd figured it, occupying the bridge was to have been the last step. Before then, both the outside team and the inside team should have been in position. Yet the rear guard had now taken control of the bridge and there were no more riders in sight. No sign of the inside team!

Then, suddenly, a tight fist of apprehension gripped his stomach. He wheeled away from the store window and froze, turned to stone. Frank James and Bob Younger, led by a third man, rounded the corner of Division Street and entered the bank. The man in the lead, like Frank, wore a beard, and carried himself with austere assurance. His identity was all too apparent.

Starbuck spat a low curse and flung his cigar into the gutter. He saw their horses tied to the hitch rack on Division Street, and too late he realized his mistake. While he was watching the bridge, he'd been outsmarted and outmaneuvered. Jesse James, foxy to the end, had circled Northfield and entered town from the east. A clever ruse, wholly unexpected, and timed precisely when it was least expected. The trademark of an old guerrilla fighter—and brilliantly executed.

Before Starbuck could react, the situation went from bad to worse. The proprietor of a hardware store next to the bank boldly approached Cole Younger and Clell Miller. He looked them over, openly curious, then walked on toward the bank entrance. Miller drew a gun and brusquely ordered him to move along. The store owner obeyed, rounding the corner onto Division Street. Then he took off running, shouting at the top of his lungs.

"Bank robbers! The bank's being robbed!"

With the element of surprise gone, the gang moved swiftly. Cole fired a shot to alert the men at the bridge. In turn, they began winging shots across the square, warning passersby off the street. A townsman, seemingly befuddled by the commotion, was too slow to move, and a bullet dropped him where he stood. Starbuck, with lead whizzing all around him, jerked his Colt and hurried to the corner. There he ducked behind a lamppost and waited. His pistol was trained on the bank entrance.

From the pharmacy, Stacey fired a shotgun blast across the street. Birdshot peppered Miller's face just as he started to mount his horse. At the same instant, the marshal cut loose from his office window and drilled a slug through Cole's thigh. Then, from the opposite direction, Manning stepped out the door of the dry-goods store and triggered both barrels on his shotgun. The impact of a double-load struck Miller in the chest, and knocked him raglike off his feet. He dropped dead in the street.

Doc Wheeler, firing from the hotel window, quickly routed the rear guard. His first shot, slightly low, killed a horse and sent the rider tumbling to the ground. His next shot went high and struck the bridge, exploding splinters directly over Jim Younger's head. On the third shot, the physician found the range. The remaining outlaw took a bullet through the heart, and pitched headlong off his horse.

A shot sounded from within the bank and one of the tellers stumbled through the door. He lost his footing and fell face first on the sidewalk. On his heels, the three inside men burst out the door and ran for their horses. Frank was in the lead, followed by Jesse, and last in line was Bob Younger. Bunched together, they dodged and weaved, snapping off wild shots as they headed for the hitch rack. The marshal and Elias Stacey opened up on them in a rolling barrage. The bank window shattered and bullets pocked the wall of the building all around them. Younger's horse reared backward and toppled dead as he grabbed for the reins. Beside him, still in the middle, Jesse bent low under the hitch rack.

Starbuck, tracking them in his sights, had not yet fired. From the moment they darted out of the bank, he'd waited for a clear shot. His concentration was on Jesse, but the other men were in the way, spoiling his aim. Then, as Younger's horse fell dead, he saw an opening. He touched off the trigger as Jesse rose from beneath the hitch rack. Bob Younger, scrambling away from his plunging horse, stepped into the line of fire. The slug plowed through his arm from hand to elbow. Jesse vaulted into the saddle, and Starbuck fired a hurried shot. The slug, only inches off target, blew the saddlehorn apart.

Out of nowhere, Cole galloped into the melee and swung Bob aboard his own horse. Once again Starbuck was blocked, and he waited as they turned and thundered in a tight phalanx through the intersection. Standing, he moved from behind the lamppost and brought the Colt to shoulder level. He was vaguely aware of the marshal halting at the corner, and distantly he heard the boom of shotguns. Yet he closed his mind to all else, his attention zeroed on a lone figure within the pack of horsemen. He was determined to make the shot count.

The riders hurtled past him and his arm traversed in a smooth arc. From the rear, the horses were separated by wider gaps, and his sights locked on the bearded figure. The Colt roared and he saw Jesse's hat float skyward. He quickly thumbed the hammer back and once more brought the sights into line. Then, on the verge of firing, the horsemen drifted together in a jumbled wedge and he lost his target. There was no time for a last shot.

The outlaws pounded across the bridge and turned south along the Dundas road. A moment slipped past, then they disappeared from view on the opposite side of the river. A pall of eerie silence descended on Northfield.

Starbuck cursed savagely and slowly lowered the hammer on the Colt. His eyes were rimmed with disgust.

Chapter Fifteen

A crowd of townspeople stood clotted together outside the bank. Unmoving, they seemed paralyzed in a kind of stilled tableau. Their faces were set in a curious attitude of horror and sullen disbelief. All ears, they listened intently as Fred Wilcox vented his outrage.

Only in the aftermath of the shootout had the full carnage become obvious. One outlaw lay sprawled in a welter of blood on the sidewalk. Another, his eyes staring sightlessly into the noonday sun, was spread-eagled on the ground near the bridge. A townsman, killed when he failed to take cover, was crumpled in a ball on the north side of the square. One of the tellers, wounded when he attempted to flee the bank, was now being attended by Doc Wheeler. The other teller, Joseph Heywood, was less fortunate. His throat slashed, he lay dead beside the bank vault. The vault door was closed and locked.

Fred Wilcox, the bank president, was unharmed. A short, fat man, his visage was somewhat like that of a bellicose pig. His lips were white and all the blood had leeched out of his face. He was shouting at Wallace Murphy in a loud, hectoring voice.

"You're the marshal! You're paid to protect the town—not to get people killed!"

"I know that." Murphy looked wretched. "Things went haywire, Mr. Wilcox. We planned to get 'em before they got inside the bank—"

"Damn your plan!" Wilcox said furiously. "Your job is to prevent such things from happening!"

"We tried to," Murphy answered with defensive gruffness. "That's what I keep telling you. We had an ambush all laid out. Then Jack Allen walked out of his hardware store and spoiled the whole thing. If he hadn't got so curious, we would've mowed 'em down right where they stood."

"Don't blame Allen! The fault is yours, and yours alone! Poor Heywood would still be alive if it weren't for your bumbling."

Wilcox made an agitated gesture with both hands. His glance shuttled across the room, where the teller's body lay slumped beside the vault door. The stench of death was still strong, and a puddle of blood stained the floor dark brown. He suddenly looked queasy and his voice trembled.

"My God." He passed a hand across his eyes and swallowed hard. "I'll never forget Heywood's face. When they put that knife to his throat . . ."

His voice trailed off, and Murphy nodded dumbly. "How'd the vault door come to be locked?"

"I—" Wilcox tried to speak, choked on his own terror, then started again. "It was almost noon. I always lock the vault before I go to lunch. Merely a precautionary measure, nothing more."

"The robbers didn't get anything, then?"

"No," Wilcox said hollowly. "Not a dime."

Standing nearby, Starbuck listened without expression. Outwardly stony, he was seething inside. Within him the full impact of his failure smoldered corrosively, shadowing his every thought. An innocent by-stander dead and a bank teller brutally murdered. And Jesse James unscathed, still very much alive. All in all, he reflected, it was a sorry performance. He'd made a monstrous gaffe, underestimating the outlaw leader and attaching far too much weight to his own assessment of the robbers' plans. In effect, he had second-guessed a tactical wizard, and he'd guessed wrong. The fault was his own, not Wallace Murphy's. Here today, men had died needlessly, and it left a leaden feeling in his chest. A feeling of abject loathing for himself. And a sense of homicidal rage toward the man who had outwitted him.

"The money," Wilcox went on bitterly, "has no bearing on what's happened. Joe Heywood is dead"—his finger stabbed accusingly at the marshal—"and I hold you personally responsible!"

Murphy looked at him with dulled eyes. "Nobody feels any worse about it than me, Mr. Wilcox. I was only trying to do my duty."

"Your duty!" Wilcox thundered righteously. "You chowderheaded ass! I'll have your job! Before I'm through, the people of Northfield will ride you out of town on a rail. Do you hear me—a rail!"

There was a harried sharpness in the banker's words. He was strung up an octave too high, and Star-buck brought him down. Stepping forward, he fixed Wilcox with an inquisitorial stare.

"Tell me something." His voice was pitched to reach the onlookers crowding the doorway. "Why did they cut Heywood's throat?"

"I—" Wilcox blinked several times. "I beg your pardon?"

"You heard me." Starbuck's eyes hooded. "There must've been a reason. It had to happen before all the shooting started; so it's pretty clear they used a knife to avoid attracting attention. What's the reason?"

"The vault." Wilcox looked ill, suddenly averted his

gaze. "They wanted the combination to the vault. When I . . ."

"When you refused," Starbuck finished it for him, "that's when Heywood got the knife. Then they started for the other teller—now that you knew they weren't bluffing—and he bolted for the door. Have I got it straight?"

Wilcox blanched, mumbled an inaudible reply. Starbuck studied him a moment, then added a casual afterthought. "Who used the knife? Which robber?"

"Ooo God!" Tears welled up in Wilcox's eyes. "It . . . it was . . . one of the bearded men."

"Which one?" Starbuck persisted. "The one about my height, or the taller one?"

"Your height." Wilcox pulled out a handkerchief and loudly honked his nose. "The one who gave the orders."

"It figures." Starbuck turned away, motioning to the marshal. "C'mon, Wally. We'll leave Mr. Wilcox to count his money. Let's go catch ourselves some robbers."

Wallace Murphy thrust out his jaw and gave the banker an ugly stare. Then he let out his breath between clenched teeth, and followed Starbuck toward the door. On the steps they halted and stood looking at the upturned faces of the crowd. Murphy's chest swelled and he appeared to grow taller. His eyes blazed with authority.

"I'm forming a posse!" he rumbled in a gravelly voice. "That gang of murderers killed Joe Heywood and poor ol' Nick Gustavson! I give you my solemn oath the bastards will be caught and brought to justice! Any man jack that wants a hand in running 'em down—step forward!"

Several men moved to the front of the crowd. Murphy began ticking off names and issuing orders. The posse members were to provide their own guns and their own horses, and report back to the marshal's office on the double. They were advised to bring along blankets and enough rations to last at least two days. The chase would end when it ended, Murphy shouted. And not a moment before!

An hour later Starbuck and Murphy led six grim-faced men across the bridge. They rode south on the Dundas road.

A hunter's moon slipped out from behind the clouds. The posse was halted some ten miles southwest of Dundas. The men were dismounted at the side of the road, and no one spoke. Gathered around Murphy, they waited with an air of suppressed tension.

Starbuck was squatted down on his haunches. In the spectral moonlight, he slowly scrutinized a crazy quilt of hoofprints on the dirt road. After a time he stood and carefully followed a set of tracks that led west, into a stand of woods. There he knelt and once more studied the sign. He touched a spot of ground which glistened wetly in the light, and smelled his fingers. He allowed himself a satisfied grunt, and climbed to his feet. Then he walked back to where the men waited. He nodded to Murphy, gesturing along the road.

"Five horses, six riders," he remarked. "That means we're on the right trail. Bob Younger was riding double with Cole when they took off."

"What was it you found at the side of the road?"

"Blood." Starbuck rubbed his fingers together. "Still pretty fresh too. I know for a fact Bob Younger was wounded. So the way it figures—he passed out and fell off the horse not long after dark. I'd guess they had to let him rest a spell before they moved on."

"Sounds reasonable." Murphy pointed off into the woods. "We're in big trouble if they headed that way. There's nothing out there but swamps and heavy timber. Probably thirty miles of wilderness between here and the next farm road."

Starbuck's eyes narrowed. "Only three horses went that way, and one of them was carrying double. I'd say it was the Younger brothers and that fourth man. The one Doc Wheeler missed at the bridge."

"You mean to tell me they split up?"

"That's the way I read it. Looks to me like the Youngers took to the brush and the James boys stuck to the road."

"Hell of a note!" Murphy groaned. "They're forcing us to choose. We sure as the devil can't follow both trails!"

"Tell you what, Wally." Starbuck's expression was wooden. "Why don't you and your men stick with the Youngers? I'll tend to the James boys myself."

Murphy returned his gaze steadily. "I never asked, but I suppose I knew all along. You want Jesse real bad, don't you?"

"Yeah." There was a hard edge to Starbuck's tone. "I want him so bad it makes my teeth hurt."

"Any special reason? Or am I overstepping my bounds by asking?"

"No." Starbuck's voice took on a peculiar abstracted quality. "Some men need killing, and his name heads the list. I reckon that's reason enough."

"I'd sure as hell second that motion!"

"Lots of people already beat you to it."

Murphy took his arm and walked him off to one side. "Just in case we shouldn't meet again, there's something I want you to know."

"Fire away."

"I owe you for the way you stepped in with Wilcox back there at the bank. Except for you, I would've been finished in Northfield. You pulled my fat out of the fire, and I'm obliged."

Starbuck smiled. "Catch the Youngers and we'll call it even." He offered his hand. "Good luck, Wally."

Their handshake was strong, and for a moment they stood grinning at each other in the pale moonlight. Then Starbuck walked to his horse and mounted. He nodded to the other men, reined sharply about, and rode off down the road.

Wallace Murphy watched until he disappeared into the night.

Events of subsequent days proved both frustrating and tantalizing. Starbuck's manhunt took him on a tortuous path full of blind ends and false leads. Yet he never entirely lost the trail. Nor was he discouraged by the snaillike pace of the search.

The trail led him first to Mankato, some fifty miles southwest of Northfield. From there, always inquiring about two bearded men on horseback, he tracked the James brothers to Sioux City. Located on the Iowa-Nebraska border, the town represented a point of departure for either Indian Territory or Missouri. A major trade center, the sheer size of the town also delayed his progress.

Finally, after several days of investigation, he discovered that a bearded man had swapped two saddle horses, along with a hundred dollars cash, for a wagon and team. The switch to a wagon left him puzzled; all the more so when he was unable to turn up a new trail. Exhaustive inquiry at last provided the answer. A wagon, with one clean-shaven man driving, and another on a pallet in the back, had crossed the border into Nebraska. He concluded that one of the brothers, probably Frank James, had been wounded in the shootout at Northfield. The switch to a wagon indicated his condition had worsened over the grueling flight.

By shaving their beards, the outlaws had cost Starbuck precious time. Once he uncovered the ruse, he set out in hot pursuit; but in the end, their lead was too great. Some two weeks after the chase began, he rode into Lincoln, Nebraska. There, in a maddening turnabout, the trail simply petered out. A day was consumed before he learned the wagon and team had been traded to a livestock dealer. The James boys had departed on horseback three days before his arrival, and no clue to the direction they'd taken. He was stymied.

There was, nonetheless, sensational news regarding the Youngers. The governor of Minnesota had declared a reward of $1,000 per man—dead or alive—and thereby sparked the most massive manhunt in the state's history. For the past two weeks, the outlaws had eluded capture by hiding out in the wilderness maze of southern Minnesota. Then, trapped by a posse, they had taken refuge in a dense swamp. The posse, led by Marshal Wallace Murphy, surrounded them, and a furious gun battle ensued. When the smoke cleared, the Youngers had been shot to ribbons. Bob had suffered three wounds, one of which shattered his jaw. Jim, with a slug through his right lung, had a total of five wounds. Cole, miraculously, had survived eleven wounds, none of which struck a vital organ. The fourth robber, identified as Charlie Pitts, had been killed in the shootout. The Younger brothers, after being loaded into farm wagons, had been carted to the town of Madelia. There, under a doctor's care, they were sequestered in the local hotel.

Upon reading the account in a newspaper, Starbuck boarded the next northbound train out of Lincoln. The trip, with a brief layover in Sioux City, consumed the better part of forty-eight hours. On the evening of the second day, bone-weary and covered with train soot, he arrived in Madelia. He inquired at the depot and learned that the Youngers were being held under guard at the Flanders Hotel. A short walk uptown brought him to the hotel, which was located in the heart of a small business district. He found Wallace Murphy seated in the lobby.

The marshal let out a whoop, amazed to see him and clearly delighted. For the next few minutes they swapped stories, with Starbuck offering congratulations and Murphy extending words of encouragement. On that note, Starbuck asked to speak privately with Cole Younger. At a dead end, he was hopeful that Younger would provide a lead to the whereabouts of Jesse James. There was no love lost between the two outlaws, and with proper interrogation, he thought Younger might be persuaded to talk. Murphy quickly agreed, escorting him to a room upstairs. A deputy, seated inside with the wounded outlaw, was ordered to wait in the hall. Starbuck, prepared for a hostile reception, entered alone.

Cole Younger was swathed in bandages. Still in some pain, and doped up with laudanum, he was staring groggily at the ceiling. Approaching the bed, Starbuck thought he'd never seen a better example of death warmed over.

"Evening, Cole."

Younger rolled his head sideways on the pillow. He batted his eyes, trying to bring Starbuck into focus. Then, somewhere deep in his gaze, a pinpoint of recognition surfaced.

"I know you." His mouth lifted in an ashen grin. "You was standin' on the corner . . . that day in Northfield. Saw you shootin' at Jesse and the other boys."

"Not the others," Starbuck said softly. "Just Jesse."

"Yeah?" Younger sounded pleased. "Well, I'm sorry to say you missed. The bastard leads a charmed life."

On impulse, Starbuck took a gamble. "I sort of guessed you two might've had a falling out."

"What makes you think that?"

"Easy to figure," Starbuck said with a shrug. "Bob was wounded and slowing you down. Jesse split up so him and Frank could make better time. Wasn't that how it happened?"

"Shit!" Cole said viciously. "You don't know the half of it. He wanted to kill Bob and leave him! I told him he'd have to kill me first."

"Wasn't Frank wounded too?"

"Yeah, but he was able to ride. After Jesse and me

had words, they took off. Sonovabitch! All he ever cared about was savin' his own neck."

"You reckon he's headed for Belle's place . . . Younger's Bend?"

Younger peered at him, one eye sharp and gleaming. "Who the hell are you anyway? How'd you know about Belle?"

"Let's just say I've got a powerful urge to see Jesse dead."

"Join the club." Younger gave him a ghastly smile. "You ain't gonna find him at Belle's, though. She wouldn't give him the time of day—not without me along!"

"How about Ruston's spread?" Starbuck watched his eyes. "Down on the Pecos?"

"Ain't nothin' you don't know, is there? Only thing is, you're barkin' up the wrong tree. Tom Ruston swears by Frank, but he's like me when it comes to Jesse. He wouldn't piss on him if his guts was on fire!"

"You tell me, then. Where should I look?"

"Why should I?" Younger said hoarsely. "You got Pinkerton written all over you."

"Guess again," Starbuck said without guile. "I was hired by someone who wants a personal score settled. It's got nothing to do with you or your brothers . . . only Jesse."

Younger regarded him a moment, then nodded. "Without Belle, Jesse's got no place to run this time. So I'd say your best bet's Clay County. He's partial to his wife, and sooner or later he'll show." His lips curled in a cunning, wrinkled grin. "Watch the bitch and the dog won't be far behind."

Starbuck's instinct told him he'd heard the truth. He thanked the outlaw and wished him a speedy recovery. Then, as he turned toward the door, Younger stopped him with one last remark.

"Damnedest thing! You put me in mind of another feller I used to know. Met him once in a whorehouse!"

"Well, Cole, I guess that just goes to show you. It's a small world, after all."

The door opened and closed, and Starbuck was gone. Younger thought about it for a time, his brow screwed up in a frown. At last, no student of irony, he closed his eyes and surrendered to the laudanum.

Chapter Sixteen

Starbuck's return from Minnesota was anything but triumphant. In a very real sense, he had traveled full circle, and the knowledge did little to improve his humor. Still, like a crucible enveloped in flame, Northfield had tested his character. He emerged with a kind of steely resolve.

Now, more than ever before, he was determined to kill Jesse James. No longer a job, it was a personal matter. A contest between hunter and hunted.

A day's layover in St. Louis merely strengthened his resolve. Covering all bets, he first sent a wire to the U.S. marshal in Fort Smith. He requested verification as to whether or not a pair of strangers, both white men, had been reported at Younger's Bend. The reply was prompt and unequivocal. Belle Starr and her husband had been arrested and tried for horse stealing. Found guilty, they had been sentenced by Judge Parker to one year in prison. Only yesterday, under heavy guard, the Starrs had entrained for the federal penitentiary in Detroit. Informants in the Cherokee Nation reported that Younger's Bend was now deserted.

Upon reflection, Starbuck decided to scratch Indian Territory from his list. With Belle Starr in prison, there was small likelihood the James boys would seek refuge at Younger's Bend. The chance seemed even more remote considering the nature of Belle's in-laws. The reward for Jesse and Frank now totaled $10,000 —and Old Tom Starr might find the temptation too great to resist. Trusting no one, least of all a renegade Cherokee, Jesse would give Younger's Bend a wide berth. As for Belle, Starbuck was mildly amused. He thought the guards at the federal prison were in for a rough time. Where the lady bandit was concerned, anything that wore pants was fair game.

Otis Tilford was Starbuck's next stop. He gave the banker a blow-by-blow account of the Northfield raid and the ensuing manhunt. He made no attempt to spare himself, and freely admitted he'd been snookered by the outlaw leader. Oddly enough, Tilford seemed encouraged. The Northfield incident, he pointed out, had decimated the James-Younger gang. Which was a good deal more than either the law or the Pinkertons had ever accomplished. By virtue of that fact, Jesse James had lost his aura of invincibility. And that made him vulnerable as never before. Tilford heartily approved Starbuck's immediate plan. A staked-out goat, he observed, rarely ever failed to entice a man-eating tiger into the open. Zee James seemed the perfect bait.

After their meeting, Starbuck caught the next train for Kansas City. There he collected his suitcase from the depot storage room, and once more checked into a hotel. A dye job on his hair, added to the spit-curl mustache, turned the trick. He emerged from the hotel in the guise of Floyd Hunnewell. Then, stowing his suitcase once again, he reclaimed his horse from the livery stable. Late that evening, only three days after departing Minnesota, he entered Clay County. His destination was Ma Ferguson's bordello.

Alvina treated his arrival somewhat like a homecoming. After nearly a month's absence, she'd lost any hope he would ever return. She was both amazed and overjoyed, and she smothered him with a childlike affection that was almost embarrassing. Starbuck spun a windy tale which left even Ma Ferguson enthralled. Over the past several weeks, he related, he'd stolen a herd of horses in Kansas, trailed them to Montana, and sold the lot for top dollar. His bankroll was replenished—big enough to choke a horse, he told them with a wry grin—and he was ready to celebrate. Ma Ferguson beamed mightily and the party got under way. Like the prodigal son returned, nothing was too good for Floyd Hunnewell.

Somewhere in the course of the festivities, Alvina broke the sad news about the debacle at Northfield. Starbuck was properly stunned, expressing just the right touch of morbid curiosity and maudlin regret. All of Clay County, Alvina revealed, was in a state of mourning, absolutely devastated. With a shudder, almost weepy, she told him to thank his lucky stars. Had he been accepted into the gang, he too would have ridden hell-bent for Northfield. And got his ass shot off—just like the Youngers!

Starbuck thought it a damn fine joke. Yet he nodded solemnly, and agreed that he was indeed a mighty lucky fellow. He'd count his blessings, and stick to what he knew best, horse stealing. Alvina squealed with delight and made him cross his heart. So he did, and she sealed their pact with another syrupy kiss. Then she hauled him off to bed and welcomed him home in her own inimitable style.

That night, the waiting game began.

A month passed.

On occasion, Starbuck despaired and silently cursed what seemed an ill-fated venture. At other times, his hopes soared and he rode the intoxicating wind of renewed conviction. His spirits were up and down so often he felt like a bronc buster working a raw string of mustangs.

Toward the end of the second week of his wait, Cole Younger proved to be a swami. One whose crystal ball was not only unclouded, but unerringly accurate. Precisely as he'd predicted, the dog was indeed not far behind its mate. Zee James mysteriously disappeared from Clay County.

Starbuck learned the details from a new drinking crony. Alvina, who was herself a fund of information, had introduced him to Ed Miller. An aspiring bandit, Ed was a distant relation of Lamar Hudspeth, and claimed to have an inside track with the James boys. He was also the brother of Clell Miller, who had been blown to smithereens outside the Northfield bank. That, in itself, lent a certain credence to his gossipy boasting.

A minor celebrity himself, Starbuck traded on his credentials as a thief. He cultivated Miller's friendship by commiserating with him over the loss of his brother. Then, playing the big spender, he treated Miller to a nightly round of drinks. With practiced ease, he quickly wormed his way into the man's confidence. And Miller, who was a talkative drunk, repaid his largesse manyfold. A question here and a question there elicited all there was to know about the clannish inner workings of Clay County. In short, Ed Miller and hard liquor were an unbeatable combination.

A couple of nights after Zee James vanished, the investment produced a windfall dividend. Sloshed to the gills, Miller slyly unloaded the latest tidbit. Zee James, he related with conspiratorial bonhomie, had slipped away to join Jesse in Kansas City. Starbuck, who was a master of subtle interrogation, plied him with drinks and prompted him further. Before the night was out, Miller had told all, impressing his friend with details known only to trusted insiders. Later, when Miller staggered out of the bordello, Starbuck acted quickly. Apologizing to Alvina, he complained of intestinal trouble, and begged off for the night. Then he rode like the hounds of hell for Kansas City.

Early the next morning, disguised as a rag-and-junk man, Starbuck trundled a cart down Woodland Avenue. Halfway along a quiet residential block, he stopped and rapped on the door of a modest frame house. His hat was doffed at waist level, and beneath it, his hand was wrapped around the butt of his pistol. According to Ed Miller, the master of the house went by the alias of T. J. Jackson. His real name was Jesse James.

When there was no answer, Starbuck went next door. He engaged the neighbor lady in conversation, and soon had the full story. The Jacksons, she informed him, had hastily packed and moved out late yesterday afternoon. She thought it a shame, for Mrs. Jackson, who had arrived only the day before with their children, seemed a perfect angel. As for T. J. Jackson, he'd always struck her as a bit unsociable, somehow preoccupied. Still, in all fairness, she had to admit he'd lived there not quite two weeks, and spent a good deal of time away from home. She surmised he was a traveling man, new to Kansas City. She thought it a reasonable assumption, for it was a furnished house. All of which reminded her to tell the landlord his new tenants had decamped like a band of gypsies. Without so much as a last goodbye.

Starbuck went away with his head buzzing. Everything fitted, down to the woman's physical description of T. J. Jackson. Yet the facts, like loose parts of a puzzle, made no sense. Assuming Miller had it correct—that Jackson was in truth Jesse James—then the sudden departure indicated panic. The natural question was why—after spiriting his wife and children into Kansas City—would the outlaw take flight. One day there, the next day gone, and seemingly without rhyme or reason. The whole thing beggared explanation.

That night, upon returning to Ma Ferguson's, Starbuck got both the explanation and the reason. Apparently Ed Miller had been wagging his tongue all over Clay County. A braggart, desperate to impress everyone he knew, he'd talked himself to death. Only that afternoon, Jesse James had called him out of his home and shot him down on his own doorstep. The killing, performed openly and in broad daylight, was a clear-cut warning. Those who spoke out of turn would speak no more—forever.

Starbuck found himself in the same old cul-de-sac. He'd been thwarted again—seemingly at the very last moment—by a queer juxtaposition of poor timing and bad luck. Worse, he'd lost his pipeline into the back-woodsy world of Clay County. Ed Miller, albeit unwittingly, had proved his most knowledgable source to date. Now, with the pipeline shut off, he had no choice but to wait and keep his ear to the ground. Yet his patience was wearing thin, and the waiting sawed on his nerves.

For a week or so, Starbuck brooded around Ma Ferguson's. Alvina thought he was saddened by the death of Ed Miller, and he did nothing to dissuade her of the notion. In his view, no man was unkillable; though he was frank to admit some men possessed the proverbial longevity of a cat. Certainly Jesse James had expended nine lives and more over the years. Still, the outlaw was now encumbered by wife and children, a grave tactical error. A family reduced a man's mobility, and tended to anchor him closer to homeground. Some inner voice told Starbuck to sit tight. Clay County was the lodestone, and he felt reasonably confident Jesse James hadn't run far. Sooner or later, almost inevitably, the gossip mill would churn to life. And someone would talk.

The break virtually dropped into his lap. On a mild spring evening, a man unknown to Starbuck walked through the door of the bordello. He was big and fleshy, with the meaty nose and rheumy eyes of a hard drinker. Yet there was nothing to distinguish him from the other customers, and he normally wouldn't have rated a second glance. His furtive manner was the tipoff, and when he displayed no interest in the girls, that cinched it. Starbuck pegged him for a man on the dodge, with something or someone close on his backtrail. And plainly terrified by the prospect.

After a couple of drinks, the man approached Ma Ferguson. She listened a moment, then levered herself out of her armchair and followed him into the hallway. A heated exchange ensued, with the man pleading and the madam of the house stubbornly shaking her head. An icy realist, Ma Ferguson was a woman of little charity. She provided a service, at a fair price, and studiously avoided any personal involvement with her clientele. The man was clearly asking a favor, and from Ma Ferguson's reaction, he'd picked the wrong whorehouse. His argument took on strength when he fished a wad of bills out of his pocket and pressed them into her hand. She wavered, locked in a struggle with avarice, and greed finally prevailed. The man was shown to a room upstairs; but the price apparently included only lodging. None of the girls was sent to join him.

Alvina, at Starbuck's request, soon pried the details out of Ma Ferguson. The man's name was Jim Cummins. A first cousin of Lamar Hudspeth—who in turn was related to the James boys—Cummins was privy to all the family secrets. Yet he was also a close friend of Ed Miller, and therefore guilty by association. Whether he had or had not talked out of turn was a moot point. Suspicion alone was enough to seal a man's death warrant, and he'd got the notice late that afternoon. Jesse James had appeared at his sister's house, where he was a full-time boarder and a sometime farm hand. The purpose of the visit was unmistakable.

His sister, when questioned, had denied any knowledge of his whereabouts. Understandably skeptical, the outlaw had bullied and threatened, but he'd done her no harm. Instead, he took her fourteen-year-old son into the woods and attempted to beat the truth out of him. When the boy refused to talk, Jesse James left him bloodied and senseless, and rode off in disgust. That evening, upon arriving home, Cummins realized he was in imminent danger. To run was an admission of guilt; to stay put, on the other hand, would merely get him killed. He needed refuge, and he needed it fast. He'd made a beeline for Ma Ferguson's place.

Starbuck sensed opportunity. Cummins' professed innocence had a false ring; anyone that close to the fire had to come away singed. The great likelihood was that Cummins knew too much for his own good, and the good of Jesse James. Starbuck thought he might be persuaded to talk.

Late that night, with Alvina asleep, Starbuck eased out of bed. He dressed in the dark and slipped quietly from the room. All the girls had retired an hour or so earlier, and the house was still. Fortunately, like all whorehouses, there were no locks on the doors, and that made his job simpler. He catfooted down the hall and let himself into Cummins' room. He waited a moment, listening to the even rise and fall of the man's breathing. Then he pulled his sixgun and crossed to the bed.

"Cummins." He stuck the snout of the pistol in Cummins' ear. "Wake up."

"What the hell!"

Cummins jerked and started to sit up. Starbuck pressed the muzzle deeper into his ear, forcing him down. His eyes were wide and white, bright ivory in the dark.

"Listen close," Starbuck said roughly. "I'm here to offer you a deal. So lay real still and pay attention."

"Who're you? How'd you know my name?"

"Who I am doesn't matter. The only thing that counts is what I've got to say."

"Awright," Cummins said stiffly. "I'm listenin'."

"You're going to tell me where Jesse's—"

"I ain't gonna tell you nothin'!"

"Shut up and listen!" Starbuck ordered. "You *will* tell me where Jesse's holed up. In return, I won't tell any of his kinfolks where you're hiding. That's the deal."

"I got no idea where Jesse's at! I swear it!"

"Too bad for you," Starbuck remarked. "That's the only thing that'll get you out of this fix alive."

"What d'you mean?"

"I mean you're no good to me unless you talk."

"You're bluffin'!" Cummins scoffed. "You wouldn't shoot a man just 'cause he don't know nothin'!"

"Think so?" Starbuck thumbed the hammer to full cock. "Try me and see."

Cummins took a deep breath, blew it out heavily. "Suppose I was to tell you? What happens then?"

"You go your way and I'll go mine. So far as anybody knows, we never met?"

"Why you so set on findin' Jesse?"

"That's my business," Starbuck said deliberately. "Cough it up or get yourself a permanent earache. I'm fresh out of time."

"St. Joe," Cummins mumbled hastily. "Took Zee and the kids, and moved to St. Joseph. That's the straight goods!"

"What name's he going by?"

"Howard. Thomas Howard."

"Who told you so?"

"Lamar Hudspeth," Cummins said weakly. "He's my cousin, and he tried to do me a good turn. Jesse's puttin' a new gang together, and Lamar asked him to gimme a chance. I thought it was all set . . . up till today anyway."

"Who else got tapped to join?"

"Besides me, there's Dick Liddil, and Bob and Charley Ford. The Fords left for St. Joe yesterday. Liddil and me were supposed to leave tomorrow."

"What's he planning?" Starbuck pressed. "Another bank job?"

Cummins nodded. "Only nobody never told me when or where."

"St. Joe's a big place." Starbuck let the thought hang a moment. "Where would I find him . . . just exactly?"

"Search me," Cummins said lamely. "Lamar was gonna give me and Liddil the address just before we started out."

"One last thing," Starbuck said, his tone quizzical. "What made you think you'd be safe this close to home?"

"Hell, that's easy!" Cummins chuckled softly. "Jesse wouldn't be caught dead in a whorehouse. Safest place on earth!"

Starbuck marked again a phenomenon he'd noted before in certain outlaws. Family men, curiously God-fearing, they never blasphemed or cheated on their wives. Yet they thought nothing of robbery and cold-blooded murder. Their morality was not only selective, but took more twists than a pretzel. It was a paradox he'd never quite fathomed.

"You lay real still." Starbuck backed to the door. "One peep before I make it downstairs and you won't have to worry about Jesse. I'll fix your wagon myself."

"Wait a minute!" Cummins called out quickly. "Just for kicks, answer me a question. Who the hell are you, mister?"

"The name's Billy Pinkerton."

Starbuck smiled and stepped through the door.

Chapter Seventeen

The train chugged into St. Joseph late the next afternoon. To the west, a brilliant orange sun dipped lower over the Missouri. The depot, which was situated above the waterfront, afforded a spectacular view of the river. Chuffing smoke, the locomotive rolled to a halt before the platform.

Starbuck stepped off the lead passenger coach. He was attired in a conservative gray suit and a dark fedora. His four-in-hand tie was funeral black, and a gold cross hung from the watch chain draped across his vest. He was clean-shaven, but his jaws were stuffed with large wads of cotton wool. The effect broke the hard line of his features and gave him the appearance of an amiable chipmunk. He was carrying a battered suitcase and a worn leather satchel. He looked very much like an itinerant preacher.

St. Joseph was located some forty miles northwest of Ma Ferguson's bordello. By horse, Starbuck could have ridden through the night and arrived early that morning. Yet he was confident that Jim Cummins—

fearful of being branded a Judas—would reveal nothing of their conversation. With some leeway in time, he had walked from the bordello and ridden straight to Kansas City. There, in a whirlwind of activity, he had purchased all the paraphernalia necessary for a new disguise. Once more checking into a hotel, he'd rinsed the dye from his hair and temporarily laid Floyd Hunnewell to rest. By noontime, when he emerged onto the street, he was someone else entirely. After a quick lunch, he'd caught the afternoon train for St. Joseph. A milk run, the trip had consumed the better part of six hours.

Outside the depot, Starbuck paused and slowly inspected the town. A historic spot, St. Joseph was settled on the east bank of the Missouri River. Originally a trading post, it later became the jumping-off point for westward-bound settlers. Shortly before the Civil War, it served as the terminus for the Pony Express, with riders crisscrossing the continent between there and California. Following the war, it developed into a major rail center, with one of the largest livestock and grain markets in Missouri. Now a hub of commerce, its population was approaching the thirty thousand mark. Which greatly compounded Starbuck's most immediate problem.

Before he could kill Jesse James, he must first locate a man named Thomas Howard. In a burgeoning metropolis the size of St. Joseph, that loomed as a task of no small dimensions.

All afternoon, staring out the train window, Starbuck had pondered the problem. However grudgingly, he'd felt a stirring of admiration for the outlaw. At best unpredictable, Jesse James had exhibited a whole new facet to his character. On the run, fresh from the defeat at Northfield, he'd performed a turnaround that was a marvel of ingenuity. By quitting the backwoods of Clay County, he had broken the pattern established over his long career of robbery and murder. And in the process, he'd left no trail, no clue to his whereabouts.

Instead, displaying both imagination and flexibility, he had taken up residence in Kansas City. A clever ruse, it had all but turned him invisible. He'd simply stepped into the crowd, joined the hustle and bustle of city dwellers. And vanished.

Yet, for all his cleverness, Jesse James had been unable to sever the cord. He was bound to wife and children, family and friends, and seemingly to the very earth of Clay County itself. In the end, those ties had proved his undoing. For no man disappears unless he cuts the knot with his past.

Still, given the nature of the man, Starbuck was not all that surprised. Apart from wife and children, Jesse James had been drawn back for perhaps the most elemental of reasons. He was a robber, and since early manhood he'd known no other livelihood. Northfield had destroyed his gang; the Younger brothers, following their capture, had quickly pleaded guilty in return for a life sentence. Then, too, the disaster at Northfield had left the outlaw leader virtually penniless. He desperately needed funds, and for that he had no choice but to form a new gang. Under the circumstances, it was only natural that he would return to Clay County. There, among family and friends, he could recruit men who were eager to ride with the notorious Jesse James. Untested but trustworthy, they would provide the cadre for a new guerrilla band. And above all else, because they were Clay County men, they would follow him with blind loyalty. His roots were their roots, and no stronger bond existed.

Even now, standing outside the depot, Starbuck had to give the devil his due. St. Joseph, although smaller than Kansas City, was yet another shrewd stroke. By not drawing attention to themselves, the gang could assemble anywhere in the town, and no one the wiser. The fact that he knew the names of the new members —Dick Liddil and the Ford brothers—was informative but of no great value. Today only one name counted —Thomas Howard.

Hefting his bags, Starbuck strolled away from the train station. On the walk uptown, he mentally conditioned himself to undertake a new role. From childhood, he dredged up long-forgotten quotes from the Scriptures, and silently practiced the orotund cadence of a zealous Bible-thumper. By the time he bustled through the door of the town's largest hotel, he was wholly in character. He positively glowed with a sort of beatific serenity.

"Praise the Lord!" His voice boomed across the lobby with sepulchral enthusiasm. "And a good afternoon to you, brother!"

Halting before the registration desk, he dropped his bags on the floor. His face was fixed in a jaunty smile. The room clerk looked him over like something that had fallen out of a tree.

"May I help you, sir?"

"Indeed you may!" Starbuck said affably. "I wish to engage accommodations. Nothing elaborate, but something nonetheless commodious. A corner room would do nicely."

"How long will you be staying with us, Mr.—?"

"Joshua Thayer," Starbuck informed him grandly. "Western representative for the Holy Writ Foundation."

"Beg pardon?"

"The Good Book!" Starbuck struck a theatrical pose. " 'I am not come to call the righteous, but rather the sinners to repentance!' "

"Oh." The clerk seemed unimpressed. "A Bible salesman."

Starbuck looked wounded. "We all labor in the vineyards, brother. Each in our own way."

"I guess." The clerk turned toward a key rack. "Would you care to sign the register, Mr. Thayer?"

"Delighted!" Starbuck dipped the pen in the inkwell, scribbled with a flourish. "I plan to stay the week, perhaps longer. Your fair town looks hospitable, and promising. Very promising, indeed!"

"We're not shy on sinners." The clerk handed him a key. "Room two-o-four, Mr. Thayer. Up the stairs and turn right. The bellboy's out on an errand just now. He'll be back directly if you care to wait."

"Pride goeth before the fall," Starbuck intoned. "I can manage quite well, thank you."

"Suit yourself."

"By the way." Starbuck spread his hands on the counter, leaned closer. "An old acquaintance resides in St. Joseph. I haven't his address, but perhaps you might know him. His name is Thomas Howard."

"Sorry." The clerk shook his head. "Doesn't ring any bells."

"A pity," Starbuck observed. "But, then, the grains of sand are beyond counting, are they not?"

The clerk gave him a blank stare. "I'll take your word for it."

"One last question." Starbuck lowered his voice. "Where might I find a peaceful spot for a mild libation?"

"A saloon?" The clerk eyed him with a smug grin. "I wouldn't have thought a man in your line of work would take to demon rum."

"On the contrary!" Starbuck beamed. " 'Let us do evil, that good may come.' Romans, chapter three, verse eight."

"Well, the quietest place in town is O'Malley's. Out the door and turn right. Couple of blocks down, on the corner."

"By that, I take it you mean a respectable clientele?"

"You might say that."

"I thank you kindly for the advice."

"Don't mention it."

"Peace be with you, brother!"

Starbuck collected his bags and crossed the lobby. As he mounted the stairs, his mind turned to the evening ahead. Saloons were the gossip mills of any river town, and he doubted St. Joseph would prove the exception. A question here and a question there, and anything was possible. Even the present whereabouts of one Thomas Howard.

He thought it looked to be a long night.

Starbuck rose early the next morning. His head thumped, and he regretted now what had seemed a workable idea last night. From the uptown saloons to the waterfront dives, he had toured St. Joseph until the early-morning hours. He'd talked with a succession of bartenders and townsmen, and everywhere he had posed the same question. The sum of his efforts was zero.

No one had ever heard of Thomas Howard.

Through the window, a bright April sun flooded the room. One hand shielding his eyes, Starbuck rolled out of bed and padded to the washstand. He vigorously scrubbed his teeth and took a quick bird bath. After emptying the basin, he laid out a straight razor and mug, and poured tepid water from the pitcher. Then, with dulled concentration, he lathered his face and began shaving. The image in the mirror was reflective, somehow faraway.

Somewhere in St. Joseph, he told himself, Jesse James was staring into a mirror and performing the same morning ritual. The outlaw, with his family to consider, would have rented a house in a quiet residential neighborhood. A newcomer to town, traveling light, he would have likely rented a furnished house. His starting point would have been—

The newspaper! The classified ads. Houses for rent!

Starbuck's hand paused in midstroke. Then, careful not to nick himself, he finished shaving. Wiping his face dry, he next stuffed his jaws with fresh wads of cotton wool. Turning to the wardrobe, he dressed in his preacher's suit and clapped the fedora on his head. The Colt sixgun, fully loaded and riding snug in the crossdraw holster, was hidden by the drape of his jacket. A last check in the wardrobe mirror satisfied him all was in order. On his way out the door he collected the worn leather satchel.

By eight o'clock, Starbuck was standing in front of the St. Joseph *Herald*. He'd taken breakfast in a café down the street, and casual inquiry had produced the name of the newspaper's editor. Once inside, he bypassed a woman at the front counter with a chipper wave. Several men, reporters and clerks, looked up from their desks as he moved across the room. At the rear, he halted before a glass-enclosed office and straightened his tie. Then he plastered a grin on his face and barged through the door.

"Good morning, Brother Williams!"

Edward Williams was a frail man, with moist eyes and a sour, constipated expression. He laid a sheaf of foolscap on his desk, and frowned.

"Who are you?"

"Joshua Thayer," Starbuck said in high good humor. "I represent the Holy Writ Foundation, and discreet inquiry informs me that you are one of St. Joseph's more upstanding Christian gentlemen."

Williams nodded wisely. "Bible peddler, huh?"

"No indeedee!" Starbuck trumpeted. "I give light to them that sit in darkness."

"That a fact?"

"Allow me." Starbuck opened the satchel and took out a leather-bound, gilt-edged Bible. He placed it in front of Williams and stood back proudly. " 'Blessed are they which do hunger and thirst after righteousness!' Wouldn't you agree, Brother Williams?"

Williams studied the Bible. "If they do, I'll bet they pay an arm and a leg for it."

"According to Job," Starbuck said genially, " 'the price of wisdom is above rubies.' "

"Spare me the sermon." Williams tilted back in his chair. "What can I do for you, Mr. Thayer?"

"A small favor," Starbuck announced. "A good deed by which your fellow Christians will profit mightily."

"What sort of favor?"

"By chance, do you publish the names of newcomers to your fair city? A list—perhaps a column—devoted to some mention of those recently settled in St. Joseph?"

"Once a week," Williams replied. "People like to see their names in the paper; helps build circulation. We collect the information from realtors and landlords. Why would that interest you?"

Starbuck opened his hands in a pious gesture. "The lot of strangers in a strange city can oftentimes be lonesome. And I ask you, Brother Williams—what better solace for a troubled heart than the words of the Good Book?"

"In plain English," Williams said cynically, "you're drumming up a list of prospects to call on. Isn't that the idea?"

" 'Whatsoever a man soweth, that shall he also reap!' "

"Cast thy bread upon the waters, and wait for the fish to nibble. Wouldn't that be more like it, Mr. Thayer?"

"You are a man of rare perception, Brother Williams."

"Save it for the sinners." Williams leaned forward. "I take it you'd like to look over our back issues and copy down the names?"

"Precisely." Starbuck gave him a disarming smile. "The last couple of weeks should do very nicely. And needless to say, I shan't reveal how I came by the names."

"You do and I'll have your larcenous butt run out of town!"

"Never fear!" Starbuck struck a pose. "Wisdom excelleth folly! So sayeth the traveling man's almanac."

Williams grunted. "The lady at the counter will dig out the files for you. Good day . . . Brother Thayer."

A short while later Starbuck walked from the *Herald*. In his pocket was a list of names and addresses, and a map of the city. One address—1318 Lafayette Street—was circled with a bold scrawl. The occupant was Thomas Howard.

Walking across town, Starbuck quickly formulated a plan. He would knock on the door, posing as a Bible salesman, and attempt to gain entry. From there, assuming he positively identified the outlaw, he would play it by ear. So early in the morning, there was every likelihood Zee James would be present. Even worse, it was possible the Ford brothers were being quartered at the house. In that event, he would simply make his sales pitch and depart without incident. Sooner or later, Jesse James would go out for a stroll, perhaps wander downtown on an errand. Time enough then to brace him on the street. Shout his name, let him make his move—and end it.

On the other hand, it was entirely conceivable he would find the outlaw home alone. All things considered, that would present the simplest, and the quickest, solution. By identifying himself, with the edge of surprise, he would force the gang leader into blind reaction. The outcome was foreordained. He would kill Jesse James on the spot.

The general neighborhood was situated on a hill east of the business district. As Starbuck had suspected, it was quiet and respectable, modestly affluent. From downtown, he walked uphill, checking house numbers block by block. Some three-quarters of the way up the grade, he spotted the house on the opposite side of the street. A one-story affair, with a picket fence out front, it stood on the corner of 13th and Lafayette. Halting at the corner, he pulled out his list and made a show of checking off names. Then he angled across the street with a jaunty stride.

A gunshot suddenly sounded from within the house. Starbuck stopped in his tracks, stock still and watchful. An instant later he heard a woman's shrill, piercing scream. Then the door burst open and two men rushed outside. Jamming on their hats, they pushed through the fence gate, and turned downhill. The one in the lead darted a glance at Starbuck, but quickly looked away. The gate slammed shut and they hurried off in the direction of the business district.

Starbuck swore under his breath. He immediately pegged the men as the Ford brothers, and he had a sinking feeling about the gunshot. His nerves stretched tight, he walked to the fence and eased through the gate. Then he dropped the satchel and warily approached the house. His gun hand slipped beneath the front of his jacket.

The door was open, and from inside he heard a low, keening moan. A step at a time, he edged slowly through the door. The children, a young boy and a little girl, were the first thing he saw. Across the parlor, standing frozen in the kitchen doorway, they stared with shocked round eyes. Their faces, like marble statuary, were drained of color.

Starbuck's gaze shuttled from them to the woman. She was on her knees, caught in a shaft of sunlight from the front window. Her dress was splashed red with blood and her head arched back in a strangled sob. She cradled a man in her arms, rocking back and forth, holding him tightly to her breast. His feet were tangled in an overturned chair, and on a nearby sofa lay a double shoulder rig, pistol butts protruding from the holsters. His left eye was an oozing dot and the back of his skull was blown apart directly behind the right ear. A stench of death filled the parlor.

Starbuck saw then he was too late. The woman crouched on the floor was Zee James. Her blood-soaked dress and her wailing cry were stark testament to a grisly truth.

The dead man in her arms was Jesse James.

Chapter Eighteen

The coroner's inquest began the next morning.

News of Jesse James' death had created a national sensation. Accounts of the killing rated banner headlines from New York to Los Angeles. The stories, based on hearsay and preliminary reports, were sparse on details. Yet the overall theme of the stories reflected a universal sentiment. The Robin Hood of American outlaws had been laid low by a hired assassin.

The hearing room was packed with an overflow crowd. Newspaper reporters from as far away as Kansas City and St. Louis were seated down front. Behind them, wedged together in a solid mass, was a throng of spectators. The majority, citizens of St. Joseph, were drawn by morbid curiosity. Farmers and people from outlying towns were drawn by grief, and a compelling sense of outrage. They were there to look upon the man who was already being labeled "the dirty little coward."

Starbuck was seated in the front row. Outwardly

composed, he was still in the guise of the Bible sales-man, Joshua Thayer. Underneath, however, he was filled with a strange ambivalence. Jesse James was dead, and whether by his hand or that of Bob Ford, the result was the same. Yet he felt oddly cheated, almost bitter. Once again, as though some capricious power were at work, he had been thwarted at the very last moment. After months of investigation, added to the strain of operating undercover, the letdown was overwhelming. By his reasoning, he'd been robbed of a hard-won victory.

Still, for all that, his assignment was not yet com-pleted. There was widespread speculation that Frank James would appear—at the risk of his own life—and take vengeance on his brother's killer. Starbuck con-sidered it an improbable notion. Frank James, in his view, was too smart for such a dumb play. On the out-side chance he was wrong, however, he waited. One day more hardly seemed to matter.

The inquest, thus far, had produced no startling revelations. Zee James, who was eight months preg-nant, and reportedly still in a state of shock, had not been called to testify. Sheriff John Timberlake, sum-moned from Clay County, had earlier viewed the body in the town mortuary. Based on long personal ac-quaintance, he positively identified the dead man as Jesse James. Dick Liddil, collared at the last moment by Sheriff Timberlake, had been hauled along to St. Joseph. In corroborating the identification, he noted the deceased was missing a finger on the left hand. The outlaw leader was known to have suffered a simi-lar loss during the Civil War.

Horace Heddens, the coroner, conducted the in-quest like a ringmaster working a three-ring circus. He was on the sundown side of fifty, with thin hair and watery brown eyes. Yet his reedy voice was clipped with authority, and he brooked no nonsense from the spectators. When he called Bob Ford to the witness chair, the hearing room erupted in a gruff buzz of conversation. Heddens took up a gavel and quickly hammered the crowd into silence.

Starbuck, with clinical interest, studied the witness while he was being sworn. He thought he'd never seen a more unlikely-looking killer. Under different circumstances, Bob Ford might have been a stage idol. He was painfully handsome, in his early twenties, with chiseled features and dark wavy hair. Only his eyes gave him away. He looked unsufferably taken with himself, somehow haughty. His demeanor was that of a celebrity.

The witness chair was centered between Heddens' desk and the jury box. As the coroner went through the preliminary questions, the jurors watched Ford with rapt attention. The effect was somewhat like people mesmerized by the snake rather than the snake charmer.

"Now, Mr. Ford." Heddens held up a long-barreled revolver. "I direct your attention to this Smith & Wesson forty-four-caliber pistol. Do you recognize it?"

"I do," Ford said without hesitation. "It's the gun I used to kill Jesse James."

"For the record," Heddens said, placing the revolver on the desk. "You shot the deceased yesterday —April 3, 1882—at approximately nine o'clock in the morning. Is that correct?"

"Yessir," Ford smirked. "Shot him deader'n a doornail."

Heddens laced his fingers together. "For the benefit of the jurors, would you elaborate as to your motive?"

"The reward," Ford said simply. "I did it for the money—ten thousand dollars."

"Were you acting on your own, or at the behest of someone else?"

"Oh, it was official," Ford assured him. "I went to Sheriff Timberlake a couple of weeks ago. Told him I had a once-in-a-lifetime chance to get Jesse."

"Exactly how did this 'chance' come about?"

"Well, like I said, it started a couple of weeks ago.

Jesse's gang was all broke up, and he come to Clay County lookin' for new men. I'd known him off and on, and he'd always treated me decent. So I told him me and Charley—that's my brother—wanted to join up and be outlaws. He took to the idea right off, and said I'd get instructions where to meet him. Course, he never had no idea we'd play him false."

"What happened next?"

"That's when I contacted Sheriff Timberlake." Ford's mouth lifted in a sly smile. "Told him I'd deliver Jesse for the reward and a promise of immunity. He went to see the governor, and by the end of the week we had ourselves a deal."

"Thomas Crittenden?" Heddens prompted. "The governor of Missouri?"

"The one and only," Ford said smugly. "He authorized me to go ahead and do it the best way I saw fit."

"There was never any question of taking Jesse James alive? The plan, as sanctioned by Governor Crittenden, was to kill him in the most expedient manner. Is that essentially correct?"

"Naturally." Ford grinned, and wagged his head. "Only a fool would try to take him prisoner. It was either kill him or chuck the whole idea."

"Proceed," Heddens said sternly. "What next transpired?"

"Jesse brought me and Charley here to St. Joe. He had a bank job lined up, and we was to stay with him till the time come. So we moved in with him."

"You refer to the deceased's place of residence, on Lafayette Street?"

"That's right."

"Continue."

"Well, it was touch and go for a while. Jesse was always on guard, real leery. Never once saw him go out of the house during the day. After dark he'd go downtown and get the newspapers, 'specially the Kansas City *Times*. But mostly that just put him in a bad frame of mind, and spoiled our chances all the more."

"Are you saying the newspapers affected his mood?"

"Yeah." Ford gestured with his hands. "A few days ago there was a piece in the *Times*. It went on about how he was all washed up, called him a has-been outlaw. He got awful mad, and said he'd show 'em Jesse James wasn't done yet. Things like that kept him edgy, and just made it harder for us."

"Harder in what way?"

"He always went armed, even in the house. Carried two guns, a Colt and a Smith & Wesson, both forty-fives. Wore 'em in shoulder holsters he'd had made special. So we just never had a chance to get the drop on him. Not till yesterday anyway."

Heddens addressed him directly. "Why was yesterday any different than normal?"

"Jesse was all fired up," Ford replied. "He'd decided to pull the bank job next Monday, and that put him in high spirits. After breakfast, me and Charley followed him into the parlor. He spotted some dust on a picture hanging by the front window, and darned if he didn't go get himself a feather duster."

"He was still armed at that point?"

"Yeah, he was." Ford's expression turned to mild wonder. "Then he says something about how the neighbors might spot him through the window, wearing them guns. So I'm blessed if he don't slip out of the shoulder rig and lay it across a divan. I like to swallowed my tongue."

"So he was then completely disarmed?"

"That's the size of it." Ford nervously licked his lips. "Next thing I know, he stepped up on a straight-backed chair and commenced to dust the picture. Charley and me looked at each other, and we figured it was now or never."

"For the record," Heddens asked with a note of asperity, "Jesse James was standing on a chair—with his back to you—and he was unarmed. Is that your testimony?"

"Yessir, it is."

"Proceed."

A vein pulsed in Ford's forehead. "Well, it all happened pretty quick. Charley and me pulled our guns, and I cocked mine. Jesse must've heard it, because he turned his head like lightning. I fired and the ball struck him square in the left eye. Not one of us ever spoke a word. I just fired and he dropped dead at Charley's feet."

The hearing room went deathly still. The jurors were immobile, staring at Ford with open revulsion. A woman's sob, muffled by a handkerchief, was the only sound from the spectators. At length, with a look of utter contempt, Heddens spoke to the witness.

"What were your actions immediately following the shooting?"

"We cleared out," Ford muttered, lowering his eyes. "We went down to the telegraph office, and I wired Governor Crittenden and Sheriff Timberlake what we'd done. Then we turned ourselves over to the St. Joe police. That was it."

"Indeed?" Heddens' nostrils flared. "And what was the gist of your message to the governor and Sheriff Timberlake?"

"Five words." Ford looked oddly crestfallen. "I have got my man. Wasn't no question what I meant."

"I daresay." Heddens was glaring at him now, face masked by anger. "Allow me to summarize, Mr. Ford. You capitalized on a man's trust in order to profit by his death. He took you into his home—under the same roof with his wife and family—and by your own admission, he treated you fairly. In return, you waited until he was defenseless, and then—with premeditation and in cold blood—you shot him down. In short, you are nothing more than a common assassin." He paused, drew a deep, unsteady breath. "Have you anything further to add to the record, Mr. Ford?"

"No, nothing," Ford said in a shaky voice. "Except

I ain't ashamed of what I done. Somebody had to kill—"

Heddens banged his gavel. "Witness is dismissed!"

Bob Ford rose from the witness chair and darted a hangdog look at the jurors. Then two city policemen stepped forward and led him out by a rear door. There was a protracted interval of silence in the hearing room, and all eyes seemed fixed on Heddens. Finally, with a measure of composure, he consulted a list of names at his elbow. He looked up, searching the front row.

"Joshua Thayer?"

Starbuck jumped. "Here!"

"Please take the witness chair."

Somewhat astounded, Starbuck stood and walked forward. Following the shooting, he had stayed with Zee James and the children until the police arrived. Later, after he'd made a statement at police headquarters, he learned the Ford brothers had voluntarily surrendered. With the killer in custody and the unsavory details already leaked to the press, it never occurred to Starbuck that he would be called to testify. Now, while the oath was being administered, he prepared himself to continue the charade. Any disclosure of his true identity would merely serve to alert Frank James. And vastly complicate his own life.

"Mr. Thayer," Heddens began, reading from an official document, "I have here your statement to the police. In it, you identify yourself as a Bible salesman. Is that correct?"

"Commissioned agent," Starbuck amended with an engaging smile. "The Holy Writ Foundation doesn't employ salesmen. The Good Book sells itself."

"I stand corrected," Heddens said with strained patience. "Nevertheless, while going about your duties, you were in the vicinity of the deceased's residence early yesterday morning. Would you please tell the jurors what you witnessed at that time?"

"A truly dreadful thing," Starbuck said with soft

wonder. "I heard a gunshot, and then two men ran from the house and hurried off toward town. A woman was sobbing—most pitifully, I might add—so I took it upon myself to enter the house. I found a lady crouched over the man who had been shot. He was quite dead."

"At that time, you were unaware that the deceased was in fact Jesse James?"

"Oh, my, yes!" Starbuck's eyes widened in feigned astonishment. "I merely attempted to play the Good Samaritan."

"Very commendable," Heddens said dryly. "For the record, however, I wish to establish eyewitness identification. Do you now state that the men who ran from the house were in fact Charles and Robert Ford?"

"I do indeed," Starbuck affirmed. "Not one iota of doubt. I saw their faces quite clearly."

Heddens eyed him, considering. "One last question, Mr. Thayer. Did you attempt to stop these men from fleeing the scene?"

"Good heavens, no!"

"Did you order them to halt—call out for help from the neighbors—anything?"

"I would hardly have done that."

"Why not?"

" 'A living dog is better than a dead lion.' "

"I beg your pardon?"

"Ecclesiastes." Starbuck smiled in mock piety. "Chapter nine, verse four."

"I see." Heddens frowned. "So you failed to act out of fear for your life. Is that it, Mr. Thayer?"

Starbuck gave him a sheepish look. "I am not a man of violence. 'Blessed are the meek; for they shall inherit—' "

"Very well, Mr. Thayer." Heddens rapped his gavel. "You're dismissed."

Starbuck nodded diffidently and returned to his seat. The inquest concluded with the testimony of Charley Ford. His story was a reprise of his brother's statement, and added nothing to the record. Late that afternoon the coroner's jury returned a verdict of justifiable homicide. Horace Heddens, in his closing remarks, laid the onus on Governor Thomas Crittenden. The Fords, however despicable their deed, were sanctioned by the highest authority of the state. The murder of Jesse James, he noted, was therefore a legal act. The verdict returned was the only verdict possible.

Then, ordering the Ford brothers released from custody, he adjourned the hearing. He refused all comment to reporters, and walked stiffly from the room.

The train bearing Jesse James' body departed St. Joseph that evening. The destination was Kearney, the slain outlaw's hometown. A short time later, Starbuck boarded a train bound for Kansas City. Upon arriving there, he immediately went through his chameleon routine. Joshua Thayer, Bible salesman, was quickly transformed into Floyd Hunnewell, horse thief. By midnight, he was mounted and riding hard toward Clay County.

The following day he drifted into Kearney. The funeral was scheduled for late that afternoon, and by midmorning the town was swamped with several thousand people. Some were friends and neighbors, and many were heard to proclaim they had ridden with Jesse James during the war. But the majority were strangers, traveling great distances by wagon and horseback. They were brought there by some macabre compulsion, eager to look upon the casket of a man who had titillated them in life, and now in death. To the casual observer, there was something ghoulish in their manner. They had come not to mourn but rather to stare.

Starbuck, lost in the crowd, was there on business. With no great expectation, he was playing a long shot. He thought Frank James would be a fool to come anywhere near Kearney. Yet stranger things had hap-

pened. Grief was a powerful emotion, and it sometimes got the better of a man's judgment. He waited to
see how it would affect the last of the James brothers.

A funeral service was held in the Baptist church.
Afterward, the casket was loaded onto a wagon, with
the immediate family trailing behind in buggies. The
cortege then proceeded to the family farm, some four
miles outside town. Not all the crowd tagged along, but
hundreds of spectators went to witness the burial. Beneath a large tree in the yard, the outlaw was laid to
rest. Gathered around the grave were his wife and
children, his mother and sister, and several close relatives. A last word was said by the preacher, then some
of the men went to work with shovels. The women retreated to the house.

Frank James was not among the mourners.

The crowd slowly dispersed. Starbuck was among
the first to leave, and he passed through Kearney without stopping. All along, he'd somehow known Frank
wouldn't show. As he rode south out of Kearney, he
finally admitted what his instinct had told him in St.
Joseph. Bob Ford, both at the police station and the
inquest, had never mentioned the eldest James
brother. And the obvious reason was at once the simplest explanation. Frank James was long gone to
Texas.

By sundown, Starbuck arrived at Ma Ferguson's.
The moment he walked through the door Alvina
sensed something was wrong. He bought her a drink,
and they sat for a while making small talk. She asked
no questions, and he offered no explanation for his
curious disappearance over the past four days. She appeared somewhat resigned, almost as though she had
prepared herself for the inevitable. At last, with a look
of genuine regret, Starbuck took her hand.

"Wish it wasn't so," he said quietly, "but it's time
for me to move on."

"I know." She squeezed his hand. "You never was

much of an actor, honeybunch. It's written all over your face."

Starbuck permitted himself a single ironic glance. "Guess some things are harder to hide than others."

Alvina gave him a fetching smile. "You're a sport, Floyd Hunnewell. I won't forget you—not anytime soon."

"That goes both ways."

Starbuck kissed her lightly on the mouth. Then, with an offhand salute, he rose and walked toward the door. Outside he stepped into the saddle and reined his horse out of the yard.

His thoughts turned to tomorrow, and St. Louis. And beyond that . . . Texas.

Chapter Nineteen

"Good afternoon, Luke!"

"Mr. Tilford."

Otis Tilford rose from behind his desk. He was beaming like a mischievous leprechaun. His handshake was warm and cordial, and he appeared genuinely delighted to see Starbuck. He motioned to a chair.

"You made good time."

"Not too bad," Starbuck allowed, seating himself. "Caught the morning train out of Kansas City."

Tilford tapped a newspaper on his desk. "I've been reading about the funeral. I presume you were there?"

"You might say that."

"Of course!" Tilford chortled slyly. "Incognito, as it were! Hmmm?"

Starbuck shrugged. "Just a face in the crowd. Nothing worth talking about."

"The newspapers estimated the crowd at several thousand. Is that true?"

"Close enough." Starbuck took out the makings and

began rolling a smoke. "It was sort of a cross between an anthill and a circus."

"Indeed!" Tilford snorted. "I must say I find it a rather disgusting spectacle. All those people congregating to pay homage to a murderous killer! One wonders what the world is coming to."

"Folks need heroes." Starbuck lit his cigarette, exhaled slowly. "Jesse got canonized long before he died. Course, the way he died turned him into a regular martyr. I understand there's already a ballad out about how Bob Ford backshot him."

"Utter nonsense!" Tilford said angrily. "In my opinion, Ford richly deserves a medal."

"I got the impression he preferred the money."

"I was right, then." Tilford eyed him with a shrewd look. "You attended the inquest, didn't you?"

"What gave you that idea?"

"I read about a Bible salesman who testified. The news stories placed him on the scene immediately after the Ford brothers fled. I gather he was the first one inside the house . . . following the killing."

"You couldn't prove it by me."

"No?" Tilford searched his face. "Wouldn't you agree that it strains the laws of coincidence? A Johnny-on-the-spot Bible salesman—working that particular neighborhood—on that particular morning?"

Starbuck took a long drag on his cigarette. "I wouldn't hazard a guess one way or the other."

"Good grief!" Tilford laughed. "I'm not asking you to compromise professional secrets. I simply wanted a firsthand account of what happened." He paused, watching Starbuck closely. "You were there—when Jesse James died—weren't you?"

"The Bible peddler was," Starbuck said evasively. "For the sake of argument, let's suppose I could tell you what he saw. Anything special you wanted to know?"

"I read an account of Ford's testimony at the inquest. Several newspapers, however, still claim he shot James in the back. Which version is true?"

"Half and half," Starbuck commented. "James turned his head just as Ford fired. So he got it straight on—clean through the eye."

"How can you be certain?"

"A gunshot wound pretty much tells its own story. In this case the eye was punched inward, like somebody had jabbed him with a sharp stick. The exit wound was bigger, and messier. Tore out the back of his skull and splattered brains all over the wall. No other way it could've happened."

"Then he died quickly?"

"Instantaneous," Starbuck explained. "Lights out before he knew what hit him."

"A pity." Tilford's mouth zigzagged in a cruel grimace. "He deserved to die harder."

Starbuck regarded him impassively. "Dead's dead."

"Perhaps," Tilford said without conviction. "On the other hand, a quick and painless death is no great punishment. A man with so many sins on his head should be made to suffer in *this* life."

"Nail him to the cross and let him die slow. That the general idea?"

"Precisely!" Tilford said with a clenched smile. "The Romans employed crucifixion to great effect. I daresay it was one of history's more lasting object lessons."

"I hear they also fed people to lions."

"Even better!" Tilford's eyes blazed. "I would have taken a front-row seat to watch Jesse James being devoured by a lion."

Starbuck examined the notion. "Some folks got stronger stomachs than others."

"Come now!" Tilford insisted. "Compassion hardly seems your strong suit. Not after all of those men you've . . . sent to the grave."

"You ever kill a man?"

"I—no, I haven't."

"Thought not." Starbuck fixed him with a pale stare. "The killing's no problem. After the first couple of times, you get used to it. But once you've shot a man and watched him suffer, you sort of lose your taste for slow death." His expression was stoic, and cold. "You learn to kill them fast, muy goddamn pronto! Otherwise you don't sleep so good at night."

Tilford looked at him, unable to guess what might lie beneath the words. He sensed he'd somehow offended Starbuck, yet the reason eluded him. He couldn't imagine that a manhunter would harbor ethics about killing. Still, by reading between the lines, a rather primeval code had been expressed. A code common to all the great predators. Kill swiftly and cleanly, and do it well. Sudden death.

"To be absolutely truthful," Tilford said at length, "I haven't the stomach for it in any form or fashion. But then, I suspect you knew that all along."

"I never gave it much thought.

"Well, now," Tilford said tactfully, "on to other things. Where do we go from here?"

Starbuck stubbed out his cigarette in an ashtray. "I just stopped off to say goodbye."

"Goodbye!" Surprise washed over Tilford's face. "I'm afraid I don't understand."

"Simple enough," Starbuck remarked. "You hired me to do a job, and I flubbed it up six ways to Sunday. So I'm—"

"On the contrary," Tilford interrupted. "You've performed brilliantly, Luke! Without you, I daresay Jesse James would not have been buried yesterday—or any other day!"

"No thanks to me," Starbuck reminded him. "Bob Ford's the one that got him. I was strictly a spectator."

"Nonsense!" Tilford scoffed. "You routed the gang! If it weren't for that, Ford would never have gotten anywhere near Jesse James. Perhaps you didn't fire the shot, but that's immaterial. Only the end result counts!"

"The fact remains, it was Ford who pulled the trigger. I don't take pay when somebody else does my job."

"That's absurd!" Tilford protested. "I'm the judge of what you did or did not do, and I say you earned the money. I won't hear of your returning one red cent!"

Starbuck gave him a tight, mirthless smile. "I never said anything about returning it."

"I fail to see the distinction."

"I'm trying to tell you I won't take any pay for Jesse."

"Then you're not quitting?"

"No." Starbuck grinned crookedly. "Not till the job's done."

"I see." Tilford looked relieved. "I take it you're referring to Frank James?"

"Only if you still want him."

"Indeed I do! He's no less guilty than his brother."

"Then I'll leave tonight. But I want it understood— you don't owe me another dime. I'll get Frank and then we're even-steven. All accounts squared."

"Come now, Luke," Tilford admonished him. "That's carrying integrity a bit far, don't you think?"

"Take it or leave it," Starbuck countered. "I won't have it any other way."

"Very well," Tilford conceded. "Where will your search begin?"

"No search to it," Starbuck told him. "I know where he's hiding, and I'll be there by the end of the week. So you just go ahead and consider him dead."

"Luke, why do I get the impression I won't see you again?"

"No reason you should. Where I'm headed, I'll be closer to Denver than here. Once it's over, I reckon I'll head on home."

"Quite understandable," Tilford said, troubled. "But how will I know for certain Frank James is dead?"

"When it's done, I'll send you a wire."

"Oh?" Tilford pondered a moment. "I wouldn't have thought you'd put it in writing."

"Nothing fancy." Starbuck flipped a palm back and forth. "I'll just say 'assignment completed' and let it go at that."

"How will I know the wire was sent by you?"

"I'll sign it Floyd Hunnewell."

"Does that name have some special significance?" Starbuck smiled. "Only to horse thieves and whores."

The trip south was long and boring. The train passed through Kansas and Indian Territory, and finally crossed into Texas. With nothing to do but stare out the window, Starbuck found that time weighed heavily. His thoughts, oddly enough, turned inward.

By nature, Starbuck was not given to introspection. He was at peace with himself, and he seldom examined his own motives. Sometimes too cynical, he tended to view the world through a prism of cold reality. Any illusions about other men—and their motives —were long since shattered. Saints and sinners, in his experience, all walked the same tightrope. None were perfect, and he often thought that blind luck, rather than circumstance, dictated which ones lost their balance. In the end, only a hairline's difference separated the upright from the downfallen. There was nothing charitable in his outlook, for he'd discovered that rose-tinted glasses merely distorted the truth. His cynicism was simply a by-product of unclouded observation.

Yet, with time to reflect, he was struck by a queer sentiment. The more he examined it, the more he realized it was wholly out of character. He survived at his trade by virtue of the fact that he gave no man the benefit of the doubt. Still, however sardonic his attitude, a worm of doubt had begun gnawing at his certainty. He was having second thoughts about Frank James.

Not at all comfortable with the feeling, he found it growing more acute as the train rattled toward Fort

Worth. He ruminated on their one meeting, a brief exchange of words at Ma Ferguson's whorehouse. He'd sensed that Frank James was a man of some decency. Even then, under the strained circumstances, the eldest James brother had seemed curiously unlike the other members of the gang. Some intangible quality—a mix of honor and conscience—had shown through the hard exterior. None of which fitted with the known facts. The man was an outlaw and a killer, one who lived by the gun. Quoting Shakespeare scarcely absolved him of his crimes.

All the same, Starbuck had found him eminently likable. And that was perhaps the most troubling aspect of the whole affair. His instincts told him Frank James hadn't slipped off the tightrope. Instead, he'd been pulled down by Jesse and the Youngers. Viewed from that perspective, he was a victim of blood relations and bad luck. Still, no man was victimized without his cooperation. Weakness of character was hardly an excuse for murder. Nor was it sufficient reason to grant the murderer a reprieve. And Frank James was known to have killed at least three men.

Stewing on it, Starbuck played the devil's advocate. He argued both sides, and in the end he worked himself into a dicey position. On the one hand, the last survivor of the James-Younger gang most assuredly deserved killing. On the other, Starbuck was no longer certain he *wanted* to kill Frank James. His sense of duty was in sharp conflict with his personal feelings. Which was a pretty pickle for someone in the detective business. A manhunter with sentiment!

He finally laughed himself out of the notion. On the Pecos, there would be no time for such damn-fool nonsense. Otherwise the damn fool—not Frank James—would get himself killed. And that, indeed, was a personal sentiment.

With brief layovers in Fort Worth and San Angelo, Starbuck slowly worked his way westward. By the fifth day, he'd switched to horseback, and that evening he rode into Fort Stockton. There, posing as a saddle-tramp looking for work, he drifted into the local watering hole. His questions aroused no suspicions, and within the hour he struck paydirt. Tom Ruston's ranch lay in the shadow of Table Top Mountain, along a winding stretch of the Pecos. He estimated it was less than a day's ride away.

By dusk the next evening, he had located the spread. Ruston used a Running R brand, and the cows on his range were easily spotted. The land was dotted with cholla cactus and prickly pear, and beyond the river a range of mountains jutted skyward like white-capped sentinels. Far to the northeast lay the Staked Plains, and some seventy miles south was the Rio Grande and the Mexican border. It was remote and isolated, literally out in the middle of nowhere. A perfect hideout for an outlaw from Missouri.

Starbuck camped that night within sight of the ranch compound. When dawn peeled back the darkness, he was squatted in an arroyo not thirty yards from the main house. Off to one side, purple blemishes in the gathering light, were a cook shack and a small bunkhouse. He watched, curbing his impatience, while the outfit slowly came to life. As the sun crested the distant mountains, a man emerged from the main house and walked toward the cook shack. He took the man to be Tom Ruston, and that assumption was borne out several minutes later. The rancher led a crew of cowhands from the cook shack, and moved directly to a large corral. There, the men roped ponies out of the remuda, and saddled up for the day's work. With Ruston at the head of the column, they mounted and rode south along the river. Apart from the cook, that left no one on the place except Ruston's wife. And Frank James.

Starbuck scrambled out of the arroyo and circled the house from the rear. At the corner, he paused, searching the compound one last time, and pulled his sixgun. Then he edged cautiously along the front wall, and halted beside the door. Inside, he saw a dark-haired woman washing dishes at the sink. Beyond the living area, there was a short hallway with doors opening onto two bedrooms. No one else was in sight.

One eye on the hall, Starbuck stepped through the door. He ghosted across the room, approaching the woman from behind. Suddenly she turned, reaching out for a dish towel, and saw him. She gasped, and her eyes went wide with terror. Her mouth ovaled, on the verge of a scream, and he had no choice. His left hand struck out in a shadowy movement and clouted her upside the jaw. She hit the sink, scattering dishes, and dropped to the floor. He wheeled and strode swiftly to the hallway entrance.

"Martha?"

A voice sounded from one of the bedrooms. Starbuck stopped cold, hugging the wall. He thumbed the hammer on the Colt, and waited.

"Hey, Martha!" The voice was familiar, but strangely weak. "What's all the noise?"

Starbuck would later wonder what made him speak out. He could have waited until curiosity brought the outlaw through the door and ended it there. Instead, he called down the hallway. "Hello, Frank!"

There was a beat of hesitation. "Who's that?"

"The law," Starbuck answered. "I've come to take you in."

"You figure to manage that all by yourself?"

"No need to stall," Starbuck advised him. "Ruston and his boys already rode off. It's just you and me."

"What makes you think I'll go peaceable?"

"Because if you don't, I'll kill you."

"So what?" Frank shouted hoarsely. "I'd just as soon die here as get hung in Missouri!"

"Think on it a minute! With a slick lawyer—especially now that Jesse's dead—you might have a chance in court. With me, you've got no chance at all. It'll end here and now!"

"Mister, you're dreaming! I'd never make it to trial

back home! Somebody would get me the same way they got Jesse—only easier!"

"No," Starbuck assured him earnestly. "I'll get you there in one piece, and I'll see to it you get a fair trial. You've got my word on it, Frank. No one will kill you!"

The intensity of Starbuck's voice gave his words a ring of prophecy. A leaden stillness descended over the house, and for a while he thought Frank wouldn't respond. Then, abruptly, a revolver sailed through the door and bounced across the floor.

"There's my gun! I've quit the fight!"

Starbuck eased down the hallway. He went to one knee and took a quick peek through the door. Then he slowly rose and moved into the bedroom. He saw that his instinct hadn't played him false.

Frank James lay slack and unmoving on the bed. Ugly lines strained his face, and his eyes were oddly vacant. His breathing was labored, lungs pumping like a bellows. He looked worn and haggard, older than his years.

"Frank." Starbuck nodded, quickly holstered the Colt. "What ails you? You look a little green around the gills."

"Don't worry." Frank tried to smile, a tortured smile. "I won't die on you. Got a touch of consumption, that's all."

"I'd say that's enough."

"Yeah, it wouldn't have been much of a fight, would it?"

Starbuck had a sudden vision of hell. He saw himself killing a bedridden invalid, not a bayed outlaw. The sight turned his guts to stone.

He silently blessed Frank James for throwing in the towel. And his gun.

Chapter Twenty

" 'Our virtues would be proud if our faults whipped them not.' "

Starbruck smiled. "Before we're finished, you'll have me spouting Shakespeare."

"It's like tobacco." Frank gestured with his pipe. "Once you've got the habit, it's hard to break."

"How'd you get the habit to start with?"

"Well, I never had much formal education. But I got a taste of Shakespeare in school, and I was always impressed by his eloquent way with words. He said things lots better than I ever could."

"Like the one you just quoted?"

"Yes." Frank stared out the train window, silent a moment. "Believe it or not, I've always considered myself a virtuous man. Does that sound strange, Luke?"

Starbuck considered the thought. Over the past month, he'd found Frank James to be a man of his word. After surrendering, the outlaw had convinced

Tom Ruston to abide by his decision. The rancher acceded, and thereafter Starbuck had been treated like a guest. In time, Martha Ruston even forgave him the blow upside her jaw.

Their common concern was Frank James. For some years, he had been afflicted with a mild case of tuberculosis. His condition worsened after Northfield, aggravated by the desperate flight and a bullet wound in the leg. When captured by Starbuck, he'd still been weak and frail. Travel was out of the question, and Starbuck had agreed to wait until he'd recuperated. Another month of bed rest—and Martha Ruston's cooking—had put him back on his feet. He was wasted and stooped, a pale shadow of his former self; but he seemed somehow relieved that the running was over at last. Four days ago he had expressed the wish to get on with the business of formal surrender. Starbuck readily approved, and they had entrained for Missouri. Their destination was Jefferson City, the state capital.

Tonight, rattling across the Missouri countryside, Frank James had turned reflective. Starbuck detected a melancholy note in his voice, and sensed he was filled with mixed emotions. With relief, there was also the uncertainty of what lay ahead. Under the circumstances, it seemed natural he would look backward in time. Tomorrow would mark the beginning of the end.

"Virtue's a funny thing," Starbuck said at length. "I guess we all see something different when we look in a mirror."

"No need to ask how a jury will see it."

"Don't sell yourself short. I'd say the odds are fifty-fifty, maybe better."

Frank gave him a tired smile. "Well, however it works out, I'm just glad it's over. I haven't known a day of peace since the war ended. Always looking over my shoulder, afraid to sleep without a gun close at hand. No one could understand what that kind of life does to a man. Not unless he'd lived it himself."

"I've got a fair idea," Starbuck said slowly. "Course, I was on the other side of the fence. So it's not exactly the same thing."

"God!" Frank laughed suddenly. "When I think back to that night at Ma Ferguson's! It's still hard to believe you and that walleyed horse thief are one and the same."

Starbuck shrugged it off. "All part of working under-cover . . . tricks of the trade."

"You fooled us good," Frank confessed. "After Northfield, Jesse knew we'd been euchred somehow. But I wouldn't have suspected you in a thousand years."

"No hard feelings?" Starbuck inquired. "I reckon you know by now there wasn't anything personal in-volved."

"Perish the thought," Frank said, grinning. "You were hired to do a job, and you did it. I'm just glad you never joined the Pinkertons."

"No chance of that," Starbuck chuckled. "I'm not much for crowds."

"I'd be the first to admit you did very well on your own. I swore I'd never be taken alive—and look at me now!"

Starbuck nodded, watching him. "You're recon-ciled to it, then? No regrets?"

"Only one."

"What's that?"

"The Bard said it best." Frank's eyes took on a dis-tant look. " 'For mine own part, I could be well con-tent to entertain the lag-end of my life with quiet hours.' "

"Like I told you, the odds are fifty-fifty."

"I wish I believed that as much as you do, Luke."

There seemed nothing more to say. Frank slumped lower in his seat and soon drifted off in an uneasy sleep. Starbuck sat for a long while staring out the window.

Early next morning the train pulled into Jefferson City.

From the depot, Starbuck and Frank James took a hansom cab to the state capitol. A domed structure, the building stood on a bluff overlooking the Missouri River. The view was panoramic, and under different circumstances would have rated a second look. Neither of them paid the slightest attention. Together, they mounted the marble steps and entered the main corridor.

A capitol guard directed them to the second floor. Upstairs, they circled the rotunda and walked directly to the governor's office. An appointments secretary, seated at a desk in the anteroom, looked up as they entered. His smile was at once pleasant and officious.

"Good morning, gentlemen."

"Morning," Starbuck said, removing his hat. "I'd like to see Governor Crittenden."

"And your name, sir?"

"Luke Starbuck."

The man consulted his appointment book. "I'm sorry, Mr. Starbuck. I don't seem to find your name on today's calendar."

"He'll see me," Starbuck said firmly. "Tell him I've brought Frank James here to surrender."

The man's eyes darted to Frank, then back to Starbuck. "Are you serious?"

"Dead serious," Starbuck said with a steely gaze. "So hop to it—now!"

The man bolted from his chair and hurried through the door to an inner office. Several minutes elapsed, then the door creaked open. The appointments secretary poked his head into the anteroom.

"Mr. Starbuck," he said weakly. "The governor wants to know if Mr. James is armed?"

"No." Starbuck fanned his coat aside, revealing

the holstered Colt. "But I am, and I know how to use it. Tell the governor he's in no danger."

"Very well." The door swung open. "You may come in."

Governor Thomas Crittenden was seated behind a massive walnut desk. A tall man, with glacial eyes and a hawklike nose, he appraised them with a cool look. Then he glanced past them, nodding to his appointments secretary. The door closed, and he motioned them closer.

"You should be informed," he said curtly, "that I have sent for the capitol guards. In the event you attempt violence, you will never leave this room alive."

Starbuck, with Frank at his side, halted in front of the desk. He fixed the governor with a wintry smile. "You can call off the dogs. Frank means you no harm."

"Are you a law officer, Mr. Starbuck?"

"Private detective," Starbuck said levelly. "I was hired to locate Frank."

"Indeed?" Crittenden sized him up with a lengthy stare. "By whom were you retained?"

"That's privileged information," Starbuck replied. "Let's just say I'm here as an intermediary."

"An intermediary on whose behalf?"

"On behalf of my client—" Starbuck paused for emphasis. "And on behalf of Frank James."

"Oh?" A puzzled frown appeared on Crittenden's face. "I understood you were here to effect a surrender."

"I am," Starbuck acknowledged. "So long as you agree to certain conditions."

"Conditions!" Crittenden repeated with a sudden glare. "What conditions?"

"For openers," Starbuck ventured, "you agree to announce that Frank surrendered voluntarily. I have his gun in my possession, and you can say he handed it over of his own free will. That ought to carry a little weight when he goes before a jury."

Crittenden made an empty gesture. "Next?"

"You agree that he'll be tried on only one charge. One murder, one bank job, or any combination thereof. But it ends there, whatever the outcome. One trial—and that's it!"

"Anything else?"

"Nope." Starbuck dusted his hands. "Those are the conditions."

Crittenden shook his head from side to side. "Now tell me, why I should honor your request?"

"I've got a better question." Starbuck gave him a straight hard look. "Why shouldn't you?"

"I don't bargain with murderers, Mr. Starbuck."

"You killed Jesse." Starbuck's voice was suddenly edged. "Don't you think the state's had its pound of flesh?"

"I killed no one!" Crittenden said abrasively. "Besides, I fail to see how that constitutes grounds for leniency."

"How about politics?" Starbuck suggested. "Would that get your attention?"

"Politics?" Crittenden appeared bewildered. "What earthly connection does that have with"—he flung out a hand at Frank—"a murderer?"

Starbuck eyed him with a steady, uncompromsing gaze. "You lost lots of votes when you had Jesse assassinated. By giving Frank a square deal, it might just balance the ledger." He let the governor hang a moment, then went on. "Or aren't you interested in serving another term?"

Crittenden threw back his head and laughed. "Are you seriously suggesting that I would barter with a villainous killer merely to enhance my position at the polls?"

"Look at it this way, Governor. A practical man knows when to bend! Frank will be tried in a court of law, and a jury will decide his fate. Which means you've done your duty, and at the same time you've shown yourself to be a man of fairness and compassion. You'll come out smelling like a rose!"

There was no immediate reply. Starbuck sensed then he'd struck the right chord. Experience had taught him that all politicians justify unconscionable deeds in the name of noble ends. Thomas Crittenden was just such a man.

"Very well." Crittenden nodded with chill dignity. "I will instruct the attorney general to proceed accordingly."

"The people of Missouri won't forget you, Governor. It's a decision worthy of Solomon himself."

"One question, Mr. Starbuck." Crittenden studied him with a keen, sidewise scrutiny. "Why have you interceded in this man's behalf?"

Starbuck grinned ferociously. "I went out of my way to save his life. I figure it'd be a waste to let him hang now."

Words appeared to fail the governor. Starbuck turned and shook Frank James' hand with mock solemnity. He gave the outlaw a broad wink.

The charge was murder.

A trial date was set, with the proceedings to be held in the town of Gallatin. There, some thirteen years previously, the state alleged that Frank James had participated in looting the Gallatin Merchants' Bank. The actual date was December 7, 1869, and in the course of the robbery the bank cashier had been killed. Frank James was charged with having fired the fatal shot.

Missourians rallied to the cause. Though there was sharp disagreement about Jesse, the barometer of public opinion heavily favored the elder brother. For an outlaw, Frank James was held in high regard and treated with singular respect. His mild manner and frail health evoked widespread sympathy, and there was an outcry to spare him the hangman's noose. Under the tightest security, he was taken by train from

Jefferson City to Gallatin. Yet, at every stop along the way, the train was met by cheering crowds. The journey, duly reported by the press, was a triumph. The last of the James boys had come home.

Clay County led the way in establishing a defense fund. Contributions poured in from throughout the state, and the groundswell of support steadily gained momentum. Several attorneys volunteered their services; but Frank James shrewdly selected his own legal counsel. Heading the defense team was General Jo Shelby, a Confederate war hero reverently admired by all Missourians. The second member of the team, famed for both his courtroom oratory and his battlefield exploits, was Major John Edwards. The prosecutor, heavily outgunned, was Robert Spooner of Gallatin. His privately expressed opinion of Governor Thomas Crittenden was not fit for print. Publicly, he theorized that in the event of a conviction he himself might be lynched. The press agreed.

The case went to trial on a Monday morning. Prosecutor Spooner, vainly attempting to resurrect evidence, was handicapped from the outset. His only eyewitness to the killing was a former bank teller, William McDowell. Unfortunately for the state, McDowell had suffered a fatal stroke earlier in the year. By default, the star witness then became a local grocer, Fred Lewis. At the time of the robbery, Lewis was seventeen years old, and his memory had apparently dimmed with age. Upon hearing the gunshot, he testified, he had dashed into the bank and spotted two robbers exiting by the back door. Following close behind, he saw the men approach their horses, which were tethered in the alley. One robber was thrown to the ground when his horse bolted as he attempted to mount. He then swung up behind the other robber, and they galloped out of town on one horse. On direct examintion, Lewis tentatively identified Frank James as the man who had taken the spill. On cross-examintion, he admitted he'd been somewhat hysterical at the time of the holdup. He *thought* the robber was Frank James—but he couldn't be positive.

The second witness called to the stand was a farmer, Dan Smoot. On the morning of the holdup, he testified, he was riding into town as the robbers rode out. At gunpoint, they forced him to dismount and commandeered his horse. Then, with a polite goodbye, they thundered away and left him standing in the middle of the road. When asked to identify the accused, he squinted across the courtroom through store-bought spectacles. He finally muttered a reluctant "Maybe." On cross-examintion, Major Edwards inquired whether he'd been wearing his glasses on the day of the robbery. With a look of profound relief, he admitted he hadn't. Major Edwards smiled knowingly at the jurors, and asked no further questions. On that note, the prosecution rested its case.

The defense called only two witnesses. The first was Frank James. He testified he'd taken no part in the robbery, and before being brought to Gallatin in irons, he had never set foot in the town. Prosecutor Spooner, attempting to rattle him on cross-examination, was unable to shake his testimony. Frank James left the witness stand to an ovation from the packed courtroom.

With order restored, Starbuck then took the stand. Presented as a character witness, his testimony was compelling stuff. Counsel for the defense wisely allowed him to tell his story in his own words. He recounted the highlights of his undercover work and the results of his investigation. He dwelled at length on the low morals of the Younger brothers and their general disregard for human life. Then he went on to testify that, in his opinion, Frank James was a man of high Christian principles and the most unlikely outlaw he'd ever encountered. He stated emphatically that Frank had welcomed the chance to surrender, and had freely embraced the opportunity to atone for his crimes. On cross-examination, he refused to divulge the name of his client. He admitted, however, that he had been hired to track down and kill the James boys. When asked why he had spared the life of Frank James, his reply left the spectators spellbound and all but reduced the jurors to tears.

"I could have killed him several times over and in each instance something stopped me. Some people would call it divine intervention, mercy accorded a merciful man. I simply believe Frank James was meant to live."

Final arguments produced the only real fireworks of the trial. Jo Shelby and John Edwards, old soldiers that they were, followed the maxim that the best defense is a good offense. Instead of defending Frank James, they attacked the state of Missouri. Their technique was to raise the specter of Jesse James. In summation, Major Edwards addressed himself to the life and death of the outlaw leader. His style of oratory was florid, and devastatingly effective.

"There was never a more cowardly murder committed in all America than the murder of Jesse James. Not one among those on the hunt for blood money dared face him until he had disarmed himself and turned his back to his assassins!

"If Jesse James had been hunted down, and killed while resisting arrest, not a word would have been said to the contrary. In his death the majesty of the law would have been vindicated. But here the law itself becomes a murderer! It leagues with murderers. It hires murderers. It promises immunity and protection to murderers. It aids and abets murderers. It is itself a murder!

"What a spectacle! Missouri, with a hundred and seventeen sheriffs! Missouri, with a watchful and vigilant marshal in all her principal towns and cities! Yet Missouri had to ally with cutthroats so that the good name of the state might be saved from further reproach. *Saved!* Why, the whole state reeks today with infamy!

"Tear the two bears from the flag of Missouri! Put thereon, in their place, a thief blowing out the brains of an unarmed victim, and a brazen harlot—naked to the waist—and splashed to the brows in blood!"

The jury deliberated ten minutes, and the verdict was unanimous. Frank James was acquitted.

Starbuck called on Frank early the next morning. Seated in the outlaw's hotel room, they rehashed the trial and chuckled at the devious ways of politicians. Governor Thomas Crittenden had indeed delivered on his promise. The Gallatin case, of all those on the books, was the weakest of the lot. Acquittal translated into votes, and for a politician there was no more compelling motive. Those who fed at the public trough understood the nature of the game. Or perhaps, as Starbuck labeled it, the world's second oldest profession.

"I never asked," Frank said after a time. "But now that it's over . . . who hired you?"

"When all's said and done, does it matter?"

"I guess not." Frank massaged his nose, thinking. "Only you'll have a devil of a time explaining why you didn't kill me."

Starbuck smiled a cryptic smile. "The way it works out, I reckon he'll get his money's worth."

"Well, all the same, I owe you more than—"

"Your credit's good." Starbuck extended his hand. "Stick to the straight and narrow, Frank."

Frank grinned like a possum. " 'Read not my blemishes in the world's report; I have not kept the square, but that to come shall all be done by the rule.' You can bank on it, Luke."

"I already did." Starbuck shook his hand hard. "Down on the Pecos."

Outside the hotel, Starbuck crossed the street and stepped into the post office. He bought stamps and pasted them onto a letter. The envelope was addressed to Otis Tilford, and inside was a bank draft for $10,000. The accompanying message was short and succinct: "No delivery, no charge. Refund enclosed."

He smiled and dropped the letter through the slot. Then, whistling softly to himself, he strolled down to the depot. He caught the morning train for Kansas City and points west.

His assignment in Missouri was complete.

Chapter Twenty-one

The Alcazar Variety Theater was hushed and still. Starbuck stopped just inside the bat-wing doors. All eyes were fixed on the stage and the crowd appeared hypnotized. He joined them, thumbs hooked in his vest. A slow smile touched the corner of his mouth.

Lola Montana was bathed in the cider glow of a spotlight. She stood center stage, her face lifted upward in a woeful expression. Her gown was teal blue and her hair was piled atop her head in golden ringlets. The overall effect was one of lost innocence, and smoky sensuality. Her clear alto voice filled the hall, pitched low and intimate. She sang a heartrending ballad of unrequited love. And her eyes were misty.

Starbuck watched her with a look of warm approval. Her performance was flawless, utterly believable. She acted out the song with poignant emotion, and her sultry voice somehow gave the lyrics a haunting quality. The audience was captivated, caught up in a tear-jerker that was all the more sorrowful because of her beauty. She had them in the palm of her hand, and she played it for all it was worth. There was hardly a dry eye in the house, and even the pug-nosed bouncer looked a little weepy. She held them enthralled to the very last note.

A moment slipped past, frozen in time. Then the crowd roared to life, the theater vibrating to thunderous applause and wild cheers. Lola took a bow, then another and another, and still the house rocked with ovation. At last, she signaled the maestro and the orchestra segued into a rousing dance number. A line of chorus girls exploded out of the wings and went high-stepping across the stage. Lola raised her skirts, revealing a shapely leg, and joined them in a prancing cakewalk. The girls squealed and Lola flashed her underdrawers and the tempo of the music quickened. The audience went mad with exuberance.

Jack Brady, proprietor of the Alcazar, suddenly spotted Starbuck. He bulled through a throng of regulars at the bar and hurried toward the door. His bustling manner attracted attention, and other men turned to look. A low murmur swept back over the crowd as they recognized the manhunter. The theater owner, enthusiasm written across his face, stuck out his hand. He gave Starbuck a nutcracker grin, and began pumping his arm.

"Welcome home, Luke!"

"Hello, Jack."

"By God, you're a sight for sore eyes! When did you hit town?"

"Couple of hours ago," Starbuck said pleasantly. "Came in on the evening train."

"No need to ask where from!" Brady laughed. "The whole town's buzzing about you. Newspapers have been full of it for the last week!"

"Don't believe everything you read."

"Go on with you!" Brady hooted. "You made the front page, Luke! Headlines and a story as long as your arm. The whole ball of wax!"

Starbuck looked uncomfortable. "Well, I reckon it's yesterday's news now."

"In a pigs eye! Every son-of-a-bitch in Denver wants to buy you a drink. You wait and see!"

"I guess I'll pass," Starbuck said matter-of-factly. "Got a table for me, Jack?"

"You damn betcha I do! Best table in the house!"

Brady wheeled about and cleared a path through the crowd. Starbuck tagged along, not at all pleased by the attention. Westbound on the train, he'd read news stories of the trial, which had created a furor in the nation's press. Worse, he had found his photo prominently displayed in the papers, alongside that of Frank James. The publicity was unwanted, and the photo would definitely prove a liability on future undercover assignments. Still, despite the sensationalism, he'd thought his privacy would be respected in Denver. Jack Brady's ebullient greeting dispelled that notion. An unobtrusive personal life appeared to be a thing of the past.

A spate of jubilant shouts erupted all around him. Men jostled and shoved, pushing forward to slap him on the back or try for a quick handshake. There was a curious note to their congratulations and the general tenor of the reception. For all his reputation as a man-killer, they perceived no weakness in the fact he'd spared Frank James. Instead, they were all the more awed, oddly fascinated and unable to hide it. There was something godlike in possessing the power to kill —within the law—and choosing instead to grant clemency. The very idea of it was scary and admirable, all rolled into one. To the sporting crowd of the Alcazar, it gave Starbuck even added stature. He was no longer merely a celebrity, the town's resident manhunter and detective. He was now a personage. A killer with class . . . and a touch of the invincible.

Onstage, Lola's attention was drawn to the commotion out front. She stared past the footlights and saw Jack Brady unctuously seating Starbuck at a ringside table. In the midst of the dance routine she waved and blew him a kiss. The crowd roared with delight, and Starbuck bobbed his head in an awkward nod. Then the orchestra thumped into the finale with a blare of trumpets and a clash of cymbals. The chorus line, in a swirl of flashing skirts and jiggling breasts, went cavorting into the wings. Lola bypassed the curtain call, moving directly to the side of the stage. She went down a short flight of steps and swiftly circled the orchestra pit.

Starbuck stood as she approached the table. Her china-blue eyes were fastened on him as if caught in something sweet and sticky. She threw herself into his arms and hugged him fiercely. Then, oblivious to the onlookers, she gave him a long and passionate kiss. Clapping and stamping their feet, the audience broke out in rowdy applause. For the first time in his life, Starbuck blushed. He finally got himself disengaged from her embrace, and managed to plant her in a chair. He sat down fast.

"Hello, lover," Lola said breathlessly. "Did I embarrass you?"

"Some," Starbuck replied with a shrug. "I'm not used to an audience."

"Who cares!" She wrinkled her nose with an impudent smile. "You looked too yummy to resist."

"Yeah." Starbuck's eyes dipped to the top of her peekaboo gown. "You might have a point there."

"Why, Mr. Starbuck!" She fluttered her eyelashes. "I do think you missed me . . . or did you?"

Starbuck chuckled. "You crossed my mind now and then. Couple of times, I even had trouble getting to sleep."

"I'll bet!" She sniffed, lifting her chin. "You probably tapped half the farm girls in Missouri!"

"Who, me?" Starbuck looked at her with mock indignation. "I was so busy chasing robbers it kept me worn down to the nubbin. Don't you read the papers?"

"Do I ever!" She threw her hand to her head with a

theatrical shudder. "God, my heart was in my mouth when I read those stories. It's a wonder you weren't killed!"

"I can see you almost perished with worry."

"Well, seriously, lover." Her mood suddenly turned somber. "Do me a favor and kill the bastard next time! I want you all in one piece."

"If it was anybody else—" Starbuck stopped, weighing his words. "Let's just say Frank James was a special case, and leave it at that."

A waiter appeared with a bottle of champagne. He poured, then tucked the bottle into an ice bucket and hurried off. Lola lifted her glass and leaned closer.

"A toast." Her voice went husky. "To you and me —and lots of long nights!"

"I'll drink to that." Starbuck sipped, then slowly lowered his glass. "Only we'll have to hold it to a couple of long nights."

"Ooo God!" She groaned. "Tell me it's not so!"

"Wouldn't lie to you," Starbuck said cheerily. "I stopped by the office and there was an urgent message."

"Just my luck," she marveled. "All right, break it to me gently. Where are you off to now, lover?"

"Wyoming," Starbuck confided. "Some payroll robber named Cassidy was kind enough to leave his calling card. A client wants me to . . . return the favor."

"It's the story of my life." She stuck out her lip in a little-girl pout. "Here today, gone tomorrow."

"No," Starbuck said, a devilish glint in his eye. "Day after tomorrow."

"That's right!" She brightened, sat straighter. "You said a couple of nights—didn't you?"

"Play your cards right, and we might even squeeze in a matinee."

Lola Montana laughed a deep, throaty laugh. Starbuck poured champagne, and gave her a jolly wink. He thought it was good to be home.

Epilogue

New Orleans

May 14, 1903

Starbuck stepped off the trolley car on a warm spring evening. Crossing the street, he went through a turnstile and entered the fairgrounds. He walked toward a candy-striped circus tent.

The sticky humidity made him long for Denver. After two days in New Orleans, he was feeling a bit worn and frazzled. Age had begun to thicken his waistline, and he'd ruefully come to the conclusion that he no longer had much tolerance for heat. Yet, for all the passing years, he was nonetheless an imposing figure of a man. He was still sledge-shouldered, with solid features and the look of vigorous good health. His eyes were alert and quick, and the force of his pale blue gaze was undiminished by time. Nor had age dimmed his zest for his work and the challenge of the chase. He still hunted men.

These days, Starbuck seldom worked alone. Over the years, his reputation as a detective had brought him national attention. At last, with clients begging him to go on retainer, the caseload had become too much for one man. In 1890, he had begun an expansion program, establishing branch agencies throughout the West. By the turn of the century, he had offices in Denver, San Francisco, Portland, and Tulsa. The agencies were staffed with former law officers, and he'd given each of the branch superintendents a high degree of autonomy. His own time was spent in the field, working directly with the operatives. No armchair general, he led by example, and on-the-spot training, rather than issuing directives. Sometimes, just for a change of pace, he took off on an assignment by himself. And that had brought him to New Orleans.

Last night, glancing through the newspaper, his eye had been drawn to an advertisement. The James-Younger Wild West Show was currently playing a limited engagement at the fairgrounds. Some months ago, he'd heard that Frank James and Cole Younger had formed a road company and were touring the country. Since the Gallatin trial in 1882, he and Frank had never crossed paths. Now, by happenstance, they were in New Orleans at the same time. His curiosity got the better of him.

Hopping a trolley, he'd gone to the evening performance. Like other wild west extravaganzas, the show featured savage redskins and trick-shot artists and various specialty acts. The star attraction, however, was the two old outlaws. Between acts, they took turns lecturing the crowd. Frank spoke on the evils of crime, and recounted details of the life he'd led with his infamous brother. Cole spun windy tales about their outlaw days, and dwelled at length on the horrors of life in prison. The finale was a reenactment of the Northfield raid. Short on facts and long on melodrama, it dealt mainly with the bloody gun battle outside the bank. There were running horses and an earsplitting barrage of blank gunfire and lots of dying men. The audience gave them a standing ovation.

Watching from the bleachers, Starbuck was struck by the men's general appearance. Neither of them had aged well, and theatrical makeup did little to hide the ravages of time. Frank was stooped and bony, almost cadaverous, with the mark of years etched in his features. Cole was little more than a bookmark of his former self. His color was jaundiced and his jowls hung like wattles around his neck. Time lays scars on men, and in their case the journey had been a cruel one. Both of them looked long overdue for the old soldiers' home.

After the show, Starbuck went back to say hello. Frank was genuinely delighted to see him, eager to renew an old friendship. Cole's greeting was civil but cool, and he quickly excused himself. Later, seated in Frank's dressing room, the reason became obvious. Cole's outlook, Frank explained, had been darkened by nearly twenty years in prison. Then, too, he'd lost both his brothers. Bob, after contracting tuberculosis, had died a convict in 1889. Early in 1901, Cole and Jim had at last been paroled. But the next year, despondent and unable to find a job, Jim had locked himself in a hotel room and committed suicide. Thereafter, Cole had worked as a tombstone salesman and sold insurance, living from hand to mouth. Not until they'd teamed up and formed the Wild West Show had he begun to come out of his shell. He still had a long way to go.

As for himself, Frank had no quarrel with life. His wife had stuck by him, and he'd always managed to earn an honest livelihood. His notoriety had made him an attraction, and he'd had no qualms about cashing in on the James name. Down through the years, he had worked as a race starter at county fairs, lectured in theaters, and even tried his hand as an actor in traveling stock companies. At times he felt himself an oddity—something on the order of a circus freak—

but all in all he had no complaints. His only regret was that he'd never had the gumption to kill Bob Ford. Someone else had done the job—gunning down Ford in 1892—and his one consolation was that the "dirty little coward" had got it in the back. As for the future, Frank was relatively sanguine. The Wild West Show was booked into next year, and the money was good. When it finally folded, he thought he might try horsebreeding, or perhaps go back to farming. He was now sixty years old, and sometimes felt a hundred. Clay County beckoned, and a rocker on the porch of the family farm had a certain appeal. There were worse ways for an old outlaw to end his days.

Starbuck considered the statement a small pearl of wisdom. Upon reflection, after returning to his hotel last night, he'd come to the conclusion it was typical of the man. Frank James was no phony, and he never tried to fool himself or anyone else. Even in the old days, he had possessed that quality so rare among gunmen. He saw things in the cold light of truth, without distortion or whitewash. And he never deluded himself about the romantic nonsense published in penny dreadfuls and dime novels. He was brutally honest about the life he'd led, and his statement summed it up in a nutshell. There were, indeed, worse ways for an outlaw to end his days.

Tonight, the thought was very much on Starbuck's mind. As he walked toward the rear of the circus tent, he marked again the wisdom of some men and the folly of others. Late that afternoon he had concluded his business in New Orleans, and the outcome was anything but satisfactory. He would have preferred a different ending altogether. Something more along the lines of that day, nearly twenty years ago, down on the Pecos. Yet some men, unlike Frank James, were bound and determined to go out the hard way. He took no pleasure in the fact that he was still able to accommodate them. Dead or alive somehow seemed an anachronism. Not at all suited to the twentieth century.

Frank's dressing room was located directly behind the bandstand. Starbuck found him seated before a mirror, applying stage makeup. He looked up with a sheepish grin.

"You caught me!" He gave his face one last dab with a makeup sponge. "Hiding all these wrinkles takes considerable work."

"Near as I recollect," Starbuck said affably, "you always had a secret yearning to trod the boards. Looks like you got your wish."

" 'All the world's a stage!' " Frank said with an eloquent gesture. " 'And one man in his time plays many parts!' "

Starbuck's smile broadened. "I've played a few myself . . . here and there."

"A few!" Frank laughed. "Luke, you're a born actor! You could've made it big in the theater."

"Well, like you said, all the world's a stage."

Frank waved him to a chair. Starbuck seated himself and took out a pack of cigarettes. Some years ago he had switched from roll-your-owns to the new tailormade variety. It was one of his few concessions to the modern age; he still preferred, and used, ordinary kitchen matches. He struck one on his thumbnail and lit the cigarette.

"Talking about roles reminds me." Frank began stuffing an ancient briar pipe. "I meant to ask last night, and it slipped my mind. You in town on business?"

"After a fashion." Starbuck took a long puff, and his genial face toughened. "Fellow embezzled a bank out in California. I got wind he was holed up somewhere in the French Quarter."

"Was?" Frank eyed him with a curious look. "You say that like he's not there anymore."

"Yeah, well—" Starbuck hesitated, a note of irritation in his voice. "I went to arrest him this afternoon. Damn fool decided to make a fight of it."

"He pulled on you?"

Starbuck nodded. "Had himself a little peashooter. One of those thirty-two-caliber jobs."

Frank regarded him somberly. "So you killed him?"

"No choice," Starbuck explained. "I had the drop on him and he still went for his gun. A goddamn book-keeper, for Chrissake!"

Starbuck was not as sudden as he'd once been. Time had slowed his gun hand, but he now compensated by gaining the edge before he made his move. These days, the old .45 Colt, still carried in a cross-draw holster, was already in hand when the trouble commenced. If anything, he was more dangerous than ever.

"Too bad for him." Frank sucked on his pipe, his gaze speculative. "How many does that make? From what I've read, you must have better than thirty notches by now."

"Notches!" Starbuck repeated in a sardonic tone. "What a crock! Bat Masterson fed that hogwash to the papers and they swallowed it whole."

"I don't follow you."

"Well, last year he went to work as a sports writer for the *Morning Telegraph* in New York. For my money, they ought to have him reporting on sporting houses. That and gambling was always his strong suit."

"Yeah?" Frank appeared puzzled. "So what's that got to do with this 'notches' business?"

"Once a tinhorn, always a tinhorn! He wanted to impress all his Eastern friends, and he needed an angle. So he bought himself an old Colt and cut notches in the handle. To be exact, twenty-six notches! Now he's got everybody convinced he tamed the West and killed all those badmen in gunfights. Spun himself a fairy tale and goddamn if they didn't buy it!"

"I take it you've got the straight goods on him?"

"For a fact!" Starbuck puffed smoke like an angry

dragon. "I've known Masterson going on thirty years. He only killed one man in his whole life! And that was in a shootout over a whore. Course, nobody would believe the truth if you told them. He's set himself up as the he-wolf lawman of the frontier and it's all but carved in stone. I think back to marshals like Tilghman and Heck Thomas, and it flat turns my stomach. They're the ones that did the dirty work, and tinhorns like Masterson wind up with all the glory. Sorry bastard!"

"Life's funny." Frank wagged his head back and forth. "All this whiffledust about the old days ought to give people dizzy spells. Sometimes I think they prefer the lies—and the liars."

"Yeah, damned if they don't!" Starbuck considered a moment. "What's the reaction to these talks you and Cole give every night? Do the crowds believe you when you tell them how it really was with Jesse?"

"I tend to doubt it." Frank's eyes were suddenly faraway and clouded. "Legends die harder than men. Jesse was killed twenty-one years ago last month, and folks still believe what they want to believe. Hell, not long ago, even Teddy Roosevelt likened him to Robin Hood! And a president's never wrong. Anybody will tell you that."

"How about you?" Starbuck asked quietly. "When you look back . . . how do you see Jesse?"

Frank gave him a humorless smile. " 'Lord, Lord, how subject we old men are to this vice of lying!' "

"Forget Shakespeare," Starbuck countered. "You're no liar, so tell me how Frank James feels."

"Luke, you heard my talk last night. I might have shaded the truth to add a touch of drama; but for the most part, it's what I say to every crowd, at every show. We robbed banks and trains because it was easy work. As for the poor and the oppressed—we never robbed to help anybody but ourselves."

"And Jesse?"

"A hard man," Frank said with a distracted air.

"Too hard for me to remember him with any real charity. I guess I just saw him kill too many people."

"I'd say that's epitaph enough."

"Let's turn it around," Frank said with a glint of amusement in his eyes. "How would you want your own epitaph to read?"

Starbuck looked stern, and then burst out laughing. "Tell you the truth, I don't give a good goddamn! I reckon I never did. Otherwise I would've chose a different line of work."

"You take that attitude and you'll wind up in the same boat with Tilghman and Heck Thomas. A hundred years from now nobody will know your name or anything about you. All they'll remember is Masterson and that crowd. The tinhorns who tooted their own trumpet!"

"No." Starbuck's weathered face split in a grin. "I'll be remembered. A whole crowd will turn out to greet me when I walk through the gates of hell."

"You call that an epitaph?"

"Why not?" Starbuck remarked softly. "I'm the one that sent them there."

"Do me a favor, will you?"

"Name it."

"When you get there"—Frank's mouth curled in an odd smile—"tell Jesse I said hello."

"Frank, you've got yourself a deal."

The old outlaw and the manhunter shook hands. Then Starbuck stood and walked to the door of the dressing room. There he turned, and gave the last of the James boys an offhand salute.

Outside the tent, a line was slowly gathering at the ticket booth. Starbuck skirted around them, idly wondering how large a crowd would attend the evening show. As he walked toward the fairgrounds entrance, it occurred to him that nothing had changed. Tonight merely confirmed what he'd always wanted to believe.

A lifetime ago he had followed his instincts and spared a wanted man. The gesture had cost him

$10,000 and the everlasting enmity of a St. Louis banker. Now, looking back across the years, he thought he'd been repaid manyfold. Some men deserved to die and others deserved to live.

He was glad he hadn't killed Frank James.